BOTANICAL SHORT STORIES

BOTANICAL SHORT STORIES

Contemporary Writing
about Plants and Flowers

Edited by Emma Timpany

Illustrations by
Sarah Jane Humphrey

First published 2024

The History Press
97 St George's Place, Cheltenham,
Gloucestershire, GL50 3QB
www.thehistorypress.co.uk

British Library Cataloguing in Publication Data.
A catalogue record for this book is available from the British Library.

ISBN 978 1 80399 309 6

Typesetting and origination by The History Press.
Printed and bound in Great Britain by TJ Books Limited, Padstow, Cornwall.

Trees for LYfe

DEDICATION

My late father, Alister, was a creative man of great
talent, compassion, and energy who excelled as a florist,
gardener, and designer in his fifty years of life.
He loved reading, believed in the transformative power
of learning, and wrote compellingly about floristry and
design. His loyalty, creativity, and dedication to what he
loved continues to inspire me, as does the memory of
his life in flowers. This book is for him.

CONTENTS

INTRODUCTION

Creating an anthology of botanical short stories is a dream come true for me, as it combines my lifelong love of flowers with my favourite form of fiction, the short story.

Deriving from the Greek *anthologia*, from *anthos* (flower) + *logia* (collection), the word 'anthology' could not be more appropriate for a group of stories about lives as varied, diverse, and global as the world of plants itself.

Reflecting the deep relationship between the life cycles of people and plants, this selection explores universal themes such as love, myth, loss, and healing. Wilderness is never far away, as a woman manages to bring a part of her beloved Welsh farm to a new home in the city in Clare Reddaway's 'The Acorn Vase', while in Hildegard Dumper's 'In Search of Monkey Cups', a group of botanists in search of rare species find more than they bargained for in the jungles of Malaysia.

The green world takes a strange and exciting turn in Aulic Anamika's 'Breathing Becoming Midori' as a scientist takes a radical step in order to truly understand the life of her houseplant, while in Rebecca Ferrier's wonderful story 'Mulch', a lonely, green-fingered woman shunned by her community decides to grow her own man.

Wild plants have long provided us with sources of food and medicine, as well as less-benign remedies that may harm rather than heal. This theme is explored in Kate Swindlehurst's powerful story 'Mercy', where a knowledge of traditional plant lore enables a mistreated woman to create a better life for herself in historical Cambridge, while in 'A Clear View' by Mark Bowers, a woman foraging chalk cliffs for rock samphire meets a man struggling to survive an upbringing as harsh and unforgiving as the environment of the plant itself.

Elsewhere, the memory of gardens created and flowers cultivated over a lifetime bring comfort to those at the end of their days. In Diana Powell's deeply felt 'Emily – Hiding in a Flower', we lie with the poet Emily Dickinson as she remembers the flowers that formed the heart of her life and work, while Priyanka Sacheti's story, 'A Homesick Ghost Princess Visits Her Home on a Full Moon Night', beautifully imagines love for a flourishing tropical garden continuing after death. Set in a seaside village in southern New Zealand, Thalia Henry's 'Nigella' is a subtle, finely balanced piece about the personal meaning a flower can hold throughout a lifetime.

In the harsh, unrelenting conditions of a Dutch bulb factory, Maria Donovan's 'Narcissus' is a skilful exploration of the industrial cost of beautifying our homes and gardens. Meanwhile, the true spirit of good gardening is put to the test in a quintessential English village in Angela Sherlock's warm-hearted story, 'The Garden of the Non-Completer Finisher.'

In my story, 'Flowers', the chance to grow flowers in a Cornish field brings two strangers together, allowing them both the opportunity to heal, while love in all its wildness and wonder is to be found in the turbulent relationship between two mismatched lovers in 'Dog Roses' by Tamar Hodes. The final piece in this book, Elizabeth Gibson's 'Stitching for Clem', shows a couple weaving a deeply happy world from the small, often overlooked things – companionship, music, sewing, and growing – which deepen the richness, beauty, and meaning of life.

I am immensely grateful to Sarah Jane Humphrey for creating the exquisite artwork in *Botanical Short Stories*. Sarah is a Royal Horticultural Society gold medal-winning botanical illustrator whose talent and creativity shines brightly. As well as using darkness and light to brilliant effect in four black and white internal illustrations, our cover design features Sarah's beautiful drawing of a passionflower (*Passiflora*). The passionflower's circular structure echoes the shape of our planet Earth as well as symbolising the cycle of life. Its flowing, flexible tendrils enable the plant to climb towards the light, and its petals open to uncover an intricate, complex, and exquisitely formed heart. This species seemed the perfect choice to represent the shared passion for all things botanical and literary you will find within these pages.

Emma Timpany
January 2024

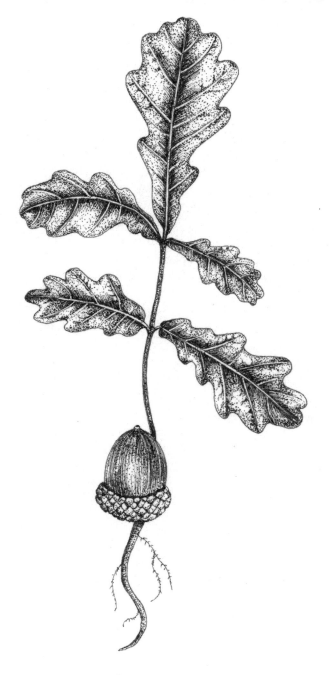

ENGLISH OAK, *Quercus robur*

THE ACORN VASE

CLARE REDDAWAY

I have to leave. That's what they tell me. I don't have a choice.

I found the acorn on the long track that leads from the road to my house. It was paved with white stones once, but now grass runs down the middle and if I'm not careful it grows tall in the summer and brushes the underside of the car. I drive the lawn mower over it when I can be bothered. I don't mind the grass, but Gareth the postman worries about his van getting damaged. I've told him a few fronds of grass won't harm it, but he doesn't listen, and I'd like to carry on getting my post even if it is mostly bills.

Alongside one edge of the track is a dry stone wall. It's still in a good state. Well, I suppose they're built to last for centuries. I often stand and look at the wall. The slabs are thick and must once have been a uniform grey, but now they are so covered with lichens they resemble a map of the world, but not a world we yet know. One patch forms the white of a frozen continent, another the speckly green of an island. There are splats of ochre and mini forests of ghost grey that sprout in the crevices. I see smears of orange, blotted with spots of black – deserts and cities perhaps. Another lichen is so dark a grey it is almost indistinguishable from the rock itself. Whenever I walk along the track I notice the spread – a new patch of yolk yellow here, a mound of moss there, new lands emerging in front of my eyes.

The acorn fell from the oak trees that hang over the wall. They are sessile oaks, twisted and bent, their branches covered in that same ghost-grey lichen with streaks of deep green moss. The track is littered with acorns in the autumn, but I have never picked one up before. Why would I?

Briony gave me the vase for my birthday. 'It's an acorn vase, Mum. You fill it with water and rest an acorn there, in the neck. It's shaped to hold it.'

A vase for an acorn. Not for a big bunch of daffs, harvested down by the stream, not for an armful of dahlias gathered in the midday sun of a late summer's day, not for a tiny bunch of snowdrops, picked when you can hardly believe they've dared to poke their heads out it is still so chill, offering hope that the wind will drop and the air will warm and there will be blue sky once again. No, none of these, but an acorn.

'Thank you. How lovely.'

When she's gone, driving straight off after lunch so she can get to the motorway before darkness falls, when her car has bumped down the track and turned left onto the lane and vanished, I put the vase back in its box and place it high on a bookshelf where I never have to look at it again. This daughter of mine doesn't know me if she thinks I want to see an acorn in the middle of my breakfast table rather than the bright purple of a crocus or the unfolding petals of my favourite apricot rose.

I love the track. The light there is limpid green, and when the sun shines it slants through the twists of oak with shafts so sharp you could cut yourself on them. Opposite the wall, on the other side of the track, the hill rises. The hill is steep but I walk up it every day, and my feet are sure on the turf path that leads up over a slab stile, up through the bracken and the bramble, up to the close-cropped turf of what was once a fortress. On the flat top, I stand and survey the land laid out below me. The tiny squares of fields, enclosed by walls and hedges. The solitary trees, oak and beech, that look like parsley heads from here. Gareth's post van, a dot of red crawling along the lanes. Dai Evans's farm, his cattle sheds grouped around the yard. His herd of Welsh Blacks move from field to field, following the grass. Beyond the pastureland the moors form a protective shield, blue as they meld into the horizon, and there in the far, far distance, is a dark line that I know is the sea.

It is the hill that betrays me.

That day, there is no sun. The wind is from the west, barrelling straight into me like a fist. It takes my hair and whips it across my skin. A sudden shower of rain douses my face and makes me feel tingle-fresh and alive.

But the rain makes the rocks slippery. I often relive what happens next. It plays like a film when I close my eyes.

It is on the way back down that I slip. I place my right foot on a treacherous surface where the lichens and the mosses have turned to slime and it goes out from beneath me. I make a noise, halfway between a shout and a groan, as I crash down onto my back. My head hits a sharp stone and the breath is knocked out of me.

When I can, I breathe in, count to five, exhale. And again, and again like I did when I was in labour. It didn't work then either. A vision of Briony as a squalling baby floats in front of me. Then I see her running with the boys along the track, racing each other, kicking a ball. They turn into the gate and vanish. As I watch them, the shock recedes.

I sit up. Good. I can manage that. I will be slow, gentle with myself. My head is throbbing from the stone, but that is to be expected. I push myself to standing and there it is: a shooting pain through my ankle when I put my foot to the ground. I test it. I can move my foot, that's positive, but if I put any weight on it, the pain is too much to bear.

I curse myself for not bringing my walking stick. For not taking more care. For choosing to walk in the rain.

It can't be helped.

I cannot manage the path on one leg; it is too steep. But I must get down. I have no means of communication. The mobile phone that my children are so keen on was left on the kitchen table. No one passes this way. No one will be here until Gareth, tomorrow morning, and I know that at my age a night on the hillside with no protection will kill me.

I drop to my hands and knees and crawl. What had been a short trek up now seems interminable and it takes an eternity to get back down to the track.

I flop onto the ground at the base of the wall, my wall, to rest.

The house is not far.

The house is so far.

I lean my back against the stone slabs and run my hands over the scrubby grass. It is then that I find the acorn. It is green and luscious, fatter than most of the plants around here which scrabble for water and life in the thin earth. I roll it in my palm. I sniff it. It smells of the earth. I put my tongue out and lick it. It tastes of tree and wood. I put it into my pocket. Steeling myself, I back onto my hands and knees and crawl along the turf to my house, my home.

'A small fall, nothing serious,' I tell Jake on the phone. 'My ankle's swollen, but I've put a bag of frozen peas on it and I've got the leg up. I'll be as right as rain in the morning.'

'Thank you for ringing,' I say to Ben. 'But there's no need to worry.'

'I *was* being careful,' I tell Briony. 'Don't *fuss.*'

I find it hard to move out of the kitchen. I find it hard to do anything at all. I haven't taken my coat off. I put my hand in my pocket and I find the acorn. Briony said that it had to be wrapped in a wet cloth to help it germinate. I put it on the table in front of me and I stare at it. It doesn't move.

I'm lying about the peas and I'm lying about having my foot up. I sleep on the old sofa in the kitchen. In the morning my ankle is like a hot red football.

It is two days before I hobble out to the Land Rover, clamber up behind the wheel and drive, slowly and probably dangerously, to hospital.

'It's just a broken ankle!' I say to Briony. 'I can manage!'

'Mum!' she says, and I can hear the exasperation in her voice. 'Of course you can't. I'm coming to get you.'

I should be grateful. I have friends whose children never call. Who visit at Christmas and send a card for birthdays. I have other friends whose children live next door. I'm not sure which is best. What I would like is children who listen. But then maybe I didn't listen to them.

Her car pulls up outside the house. My home, her home for many years.

'We need to leave straight away,' she says as she strides into the kitchen.

I've lifted down the acorn vase, taken it out of the box. I've read the instructions. I've wrapped the acorn in a wet tea towel and it's sitting beside the vase right in the middle of the table. I think it will please her, and I want to please her. She doesn't glance at it.

'Have you got your bag?'

'I've asked Maggie to keep an eye on the sheep and feed the hens,' I say. 'She'll take the eggs of course. I've got a couple of boxes for you though.'

She can barely stop herself from rolling her eyes.

'We've got shops you know, Mum,' she says. 'And I can't believe those sheep are still alive. They must be, what, ten years old?'

'Your father –'

'Mum, tell me about it in the car. I want to get going before it's dark. I took a day off work for this.'

She takes my bag and I shuffle after her, awkward on my crutches. I take the big key and lock the back door. I never lock the back door. I pause before I get into her car. The air is silken soft on my cheeks. I can smell wood smoke floating up from the valley. I can see the blue hills in the distance. The oaks are rustling.

Briony revs the car. I climb in. It smells of pine air freshener and the beige interior is spotless.

'Off we go,' she says. I can see the muscle in her jaw twitch as she clenches her teeth.

We bought the house on impulse. It was the '70s; we'd got married in a whirlwind of free love and cheap cider. Soon we had three children under four and were bouncing off the walls of our tiny flat in Kentish Town. Davey was a teacher. I had paused my job as a librarian to look after the children. My hands were red raw with washing nappies, I never got a wink of sleep, and my feet ached from pushing a pram along those hard pavements. One day I saw an ad in the back of *The Lady* in the doctor's waiting room: 'smallholding for sale.' We took the train to Wales the next weekend and fell in love all over again. A stone house with a small oak wood, eight acres, and a stream of its own, so rundown and remote we could just about afford it. We would keep goats and sheep and pigs, we'd plant vegetables, the children would run wild, and we'd be self-sufficient. This was the era of *The Good Life* after all.

It was hard work but it was worth it. Well, for us, anyway. I took a few years to get the hang of vegetables, as I'd never so much as planted a seed before. Cabbages, broccoli, potatoes, sweetcorn. Raspberries, strawberries, blackcurrants, gooseberries. We milked the goats and made cheese. We sheared the sheep, learned how to spin wool, knitted socks and hats and gloves. I made jam to sell in the market and the year that Davey had a glut of carrots we were proud to provide stock to the local shop. The children helped: digging and mucking out, collecting eggs, feeding, planting, herding, milking. Of course, as they got older, they became busy with their school work. And they wanted to have their own social lives. There wasn't much in the way of public transport but Briony still trudged the mile down the track and the lane to catch the one bus to town so she could moon around the shops on a Saturday. We understood.

One by one they left for university, and when they graduated they each went travelling before settling down to jobs. If there was some small part of us that hoped one of them would come back and help turn the farm into a modern, thriving business, we never let them know and none of them suggested it. Ben became an engineer. He works on big infrastructure projects, spends a lot of time in the Middle East. Jake went into the City, became an insurance man, making shedloads of cash. I look at him in his suit and can't imagine him under a goat, pulling at an udder. Briony is in retail. She's got three of her own shops now. She tells me that what she sells is called homeware.

Briony's car swoops through her gate and up to her front door. No grass here. Her drive is immaculate pale gravel with not a weed in sight. Her house is red brick in a street of identical red brick houses. She opens the car door.

'Here we are!' she says. 'Need a hand?' I manage to swing my legs out and manoeuvre my crutches so that I can stand. I hop up the steps and her husband, Luca, opens the door. Briony follows me with my bag. She leaves the eggs on the back seat.

She shows me into the guest bedroom. It's on the ground floor and has an en suite bathroom. It is sparkling clean, and when I turn on the tap the water gushes hot. I think briefly of the spartan bathroom at home, the old thin taps crusted with limescale, the bath that takes an age to fill because of low water pressure and ancient pipes.

'There we are, Mum,' says Briony. 'You can pop into bed and have a good rest now. Is it warm enough?'

It's far warmer than home, where the windows don't fit and the gap under the door means there's always a draught. Davey meant to fix it but he never did.

'I'll bring you a hot milky drink in a bit. We can have a good chat in the morning. Night, night!' She leans in to kiss me. It's 8.30 p.m.

Davey died five years ago now. Heart attack. He lay face down in the bottom field for a couple of hours before I realised I hadn't seen him or heard him for a while. If only I'd gone with him to put up the fence that morning. If he'd had his mobile phone with him. If he'd gone to feed the pigs first rather than check on the sheep, he might still be alive. I'd been concentrating on a batch of gooseberry jam. I was stirring it when he left the kitchen. I didn't say goodbye. I think my last words to him were, 'Don't bring all that mud in here.' 'What if' and 'if only' still go round and round my head but I suppose if it hadn't been then, it would have been another morning, another afternoon, a different field, a different season, the same outcome, rather like my fall. I miss him.

It is difficult keeping it all going on my own. The list of jobs gets longer and longer. When the children and grandchildren come home they don't want to spend their weekend mending the shed roof or mucking out the pigs. Slowly, it is all crumbling around me.

I wake up the next day to hear cars drawing up to the house and voices in the kitchen. I wash and dress carefully, make sure that my hair is brushed and smooth, my cardigan clean and the buttons done up correctly. I don't want to give them an excuse.

There they all are, sitting around the kitchen table. Ben, with his permanent winter tan. Jake, not in a suit because it is a Saturday but he looks so ironed he might as well be, and Briony, shiny and smart as always. Jake springs up to hug me, and Ben pulls out a chair to settle me down. Briony puts some fresh toast and a steaming cup of coffee in front of me.

'We need to talk,' she says.

They all look very serious as they outline the problem. I am old. Getting frail. This fall is the first of many to come. I can't cope on my own.

I protest that I can, that it was Briony who insisted –

But I am overruled.

It is selfish of me to want to carry on living in the house. It is nice enough, but there is always too much to do, far too much for one person. It is too isolated. Too far away. They all have busy lives. Families. Jobs. Social engagements.

I think of my home. The patina of our occupation layered down over the years. The willow tree that we planted by the stream when we first moved in a silvery old lady herself now, dipping her leaves in the water every spring. The pencil marks on the kitchen wall charting the children as they grew, Jake and Ben racing to be the first to get to five foot. The drift of snowdrops under the oak trees, covering the graves of guinea pigs, cats, dogs, and a lone snake, each marked with a solemn wooden cross. The summer house that Davey built so we could sit after we'd finished work and have a glass of wine together, looking out over our land.

'But you love it too, don't you? Couldn't one of you take it on?' I say. I look around their faces. No one meets my eye.

Briony shows me the prospectus. A neat bungalow, half a mile from her house. It has a garden, compact, flat, easy to manage, all enclosed by a brand new six-foot wooden fence.

'We can paint the fence, Mum, whatever colour you want,' she says.

The inside is open plan. A new kitchen. A wet room, whatever that is. A large bedroom with a wardrobe.

'What can you see when you look out of the window?' I say.

'Does it matter?' says Ben.

I think of the hill, and the land I can see when I stand there, spooling out below me towards the sea. I think of the map of new worlds on my wall.

'Yes,' I say.

'We need to move quickly, Mum,' says Jake. 'This is a golden opportunity. These properties don't often come on the market.' And I knew that they'd cooked up this plan together.

'I want the wildness of the moor; I want to feel the wind in my hair!' I think. But I don't say it out loud.

Briony drives me home. It is all settled. I will move as soon as I can sell. She drops me off. I stand by the kitchen window.

'How about your two, Bri? Won't they miss it?'

'They really liked this place, Mum, you know they did. But they're teenagers. They're all about video games and summer trips to Croatia now.'

'And you? Do you remember how you'd roll down that slope over there, all of you, racing to the bottom? You'd come in covered in grass seeds, sneezing your heads off. And that year when we got snowed in when you built a whole family of snowmen?'

Briony rattles her keys in her hand.

'Don't forget the estate agent's coming tomorrow to measure up, Mum. Ten o'clock, he said. I'd better be off.'

She gives me a peck on the cheek and is out the door and into the car before I can say anything more.

I look around the kitchen. The Aga, the clutter of jam jars on the shelves, the pine work tops. I see Davey leaning against the sink laughing as he tells me about his day. I see him stamping his feet to get the snow off as he comes through the back door, clapping his hands together to warm himself up. I see the whole family sitting around the table, talking over each other, gesticulating and cackling and giggling. I look at that table and notice a folded cloth, next to the acorn vase. I'd forgotten all about it. I unwrap the cloth, dry now, and there is the acorn. It has split and a thread of white root has pushed itself out. It is the length of two joints of my little finger. I am about to throw it away, then I hesitate. Instead, I fill up the vase and place the acorn in it, the root hanging down into the water. I can almost hear it drinking.

I always thought that they'd take me out of this house feet first in a coffin. I take six of my best glasses out of the cupboard. I throw them one by one against the wall so that they shatter onto the floor. I like the sound of them breaking, but it doesn't make me feel better. I stare at the heap of broken glass for a minute and then I get the dustpan and brush.

My home doesn't take long to sell. 'A desirable property ripe for redevelopment,' the estate agent says. I stop doing my chores. I don't care if the fences fall down, or if the currants need picking, or that the stream is blocked so it will flood in the spring. Dai comes with his van to take away my sheep. I give the chickens to Maggie. I walk and walk every day. I go down to the stream and watch where the kingfishers swoop, hoping to see one for the last time. I go up to the hill to stare into the far distance. I run my fingers over the worlds painted on my dry stone wall. I look over into my oak wood. In Scotland they call oaks grief trees. As the wind rustles through their leaves, I can see that they are weeping for me.

In the vase, the acorn is growing. A green bud bursts out of its side and works its way up into the air. It becomes a tiny slender stem, and first one, then two minute oak leaves begin to unfurl.

Briony comes to help me pack up. She is brisk and efficient. She brings cardboard boxes, which she secures with masking tape.

'We'll divide things into sell, charity shop, dump, keep,' she says. 'I want keep to be the smallest pile!'

We start at the top of the house and work down. We label furniture and pictures, sort through clothes and keepsakes. We are in the kitchen dividing up crockery when she pulls a small plate out of the cupboard. It was her favourite when she was little. It's got a picture of Eeyore, Pooh, and Piglet setting off on an adventure.

'I didn't know you still had this,' she says. She smiles and then her eyes fill with tears. My tough, practical daughter is crying over a plate.

'Sorry,' she says. 'Silly.' She blows her nose. I stare at her.

'It's not like you to get sentimental,' I say. She looks at me.

'I'm just trying to be strong for you, Mum. One of us needs to be. I don't think you understand. I love this place. I know every stone of it, just like you do! But you can't stay here anymore!'

'I want to …'

'Have I told you about my nightmares, Mum? I get them all the time now. I wake up in the middle of the night screaming because I see you lying at the bottom of the stairs, unable to move, freezing to death, and I'm not there to pick you up. I see you with a broken leg when you've fallen down a crevice on one of your precious walks. You're trapped and in agony. And yes, I see you face down in the bottom field having had a heart attack, and there's no one to find you because Dad's already dead!'

Briony is crying properly now, big tears running down her cheeks.

'I'm terrified for you, Mum. I want to look after you, but I can't. This place is your dream, yours and Dads, it's not ours. But that doesn't mean I don't care about *you!*'

I hug her and I sit her down and I make her a cup of tea, stirring in a dollop of honey like I always used to do.

'I know you love it here. I know that it is breaking your heart to leave. But for us it is you that's important,' she says, her eyes fixed on the tea. 'And maybe you can bring something of here with you.'

She runs her finger down the acorn vase in front of her, and I finally see it as it was meant to be seen. As a way of carrying my present into my future.

Briony is giving the final instructions to the removers when I get carefully into her car. I've paid my respects; I've bid my farewells. I've packed my suitcases and they are safely stowed in the boot. I settle the acorn vase on my lap. It is in a box, protected with bubble wrap but the stem is waving free. I don't trust it in the back. I'm looking forward to it being big enough to plant on into a pot, and then, when it is strong, outside into my new lawn. I've collected two pockets full of acorns. I'll grow them one by one. I'll turn my little garden into an oak wood full of lichens and mosses and rustling leaves.

As we drive down the track I take a final long look at my wall, and then I turn away. I don't need it anymore.

I'm going to a new world that I do not yet know. But I am carrying my old world with me, here, in an acorn vase sitting in a box on my lap.

MERCY

KATE SWINDLEHURST

She didn't much care for her name. Had her mother thought her a scourge or a blessing? Mercy was never sure. Always, though, she felt the weight of the two syllables on her skewed frame: Mer-see, the first remembered as a sound that shaped the lips into a sneer, a rhyme for 'slur' or 'burr', the second a shrinking, craving forgiveness for who knew what transgression?

Mercy shifted on the wooden stool, raised and lowered her aching shoulders. Then she stood, removed two large stones from the ledge above her head and lifted off the slate that covered the opening, letting in the fetid air of the Borough, rotting waste and soot, and – she sniffed – there, a gust of clean March wind. She turned back to the hearth and checked the contents of the kettle, poking at the mixture with a stick. A little longer, time enough for the wintry sun to move into the square of sky through what served as a window. Although she could not hear the rattle of the kettle, she felt the vibrations along the stick, saw the honeyed water bubble round the roots; good enough. When she deemed them done by checking for tenderness, she would drain the liquid into a clean pan to cool. The roots would be mashed and added to the bread dough proving in a basin above the hearth. With a practised eye and a sure touch, she knew what was sufficient to soothe a flatulent stomach without violent purging. The baker, greedy always though slow to admit to his weakness, would pay her well. She inhaled deeply, closing her eyes.

The room, one of four below ground level, was at the end of a narrow corridor. Little more than a cupboard, but the best of them if you wished to be safe from prying eyes. Sometimes she would catch sight of a face upside down peering in through the opening, the body bent in two like a hairpin, before she chased them off with a broom. For the most part, since she had left behind her old life in the hut by the fen and arrived at the foot of Castle Hill, she was left to her own devices. No one had reason to follow the passage to its end apart from Mercy herself and the girl who shared her bed, a slip of a thing who came and went without a word.

Before leaving the room or when she was working, Mercy replaced the slate, wedging it in place with the stones. On either side of the opening were rows of rough wooden shelves where she stored her few possessions and the stuff of her trade: bunches of dried thyme and rosemary, lavender and rue, vials of juniper oil and wormwood, barks and powders, roots and bulbs. There were twists of brown paper, too, marked with charcoal lines and crosses to record the seeds within. Positioned on an outside wall, the shelves were good for storing leaves and berries, although she needed to keep a weather eye out for damp. Next to the fireplace was a cot covered with the quilt that had belonged to her grandmother. And beneath the bed, hidden by the counterpane, trays of newly planted seeds.

Mercy leant over the pan, sucking in the spicy scent. Then she sat back, rubbed her hands along her forearms and up over her neck and shoulders, massaging the base of her neck where the splintered bone had set crooked and which no amount of flixweed would mend. On days when she longed for a kind word or a gentle touch, she made herself remember those nights at the start of winter two years past, when any small irritation, even smoke billowing from the clogged chimney, would combine with the drink to fuel his rage. He beat her until she learnt to stifle her screams.

A Dream

She is feeling her way in the dark, groping through an underworld of souls mired in the filth of the living. Which is she, quick or dead? Eyes wide, she sees nothing. She tries to stop her nose against the stench: rancid meat, smoke, sweat, and excrement, tries to shield her limbs from the rocks which encroach on her path. The taste of him fills her mouth, seeps down into her throat. Her head throbs: there is a sticky place on the side of her face. And above all the din, louder and louder until it drowns out all other senses: the spit and crackle of the fire, the thud of his fists, the rattle of the belt, her protests. And the names he calls her, cruelties spilling out of him like bile, settling on her skin like sores. Her hands squeeze tight over her ears. Afterwards, she shakes her head, but nothing can penetrate the silence.

Mercy closed the door behind her and hurried along the passageway and up the steps onto the street, the burlap bag across one shoulder. She carried the tin of bread in both hands, wary of local boys on the lookout for a free feast. Already the sun was low but, if she was quick, she would catch the last baking of the day, watching the loaf into the oven and collecting the stale crusts and nub ends the baker would never sell, along with the handful of coins he grudgingly offered. Then she walked down the hill towards the college and through the courtyard to the top of a weathered brick staircase.

A pause for breath at the wooden door. Mercy traced the outline of the letters on the metal plate with a finger: his name, the man had explained on the first morning when she had knocked once, asking for work. And below the name, the single word, 'Botany'. She knocked twice now, the second time for luck, though she supposed he had come to know this as her greeting, and let herself in: dust in the air, the must of paper, a trace of coffee, and smoke. A few coals glowed in the grate. His shoulders rounded over his books and papers, he remained with his back to her, right hand raised in a gesture she had learnt meant 'Do not interrupt'. Mercy walked through to the chamber, scooping up clothes strewn across floor and furniture, along with the pile of soiled linen by the bed. She crossed to the window, pushing open the casement. Below, young men walked the lawns, alone or in twos and threes, their gowns flapping like crows' wings. Beyond the grass, a bush covered in pink flowers stretched upwards, dancing in the wind. Now a disturbance moved the air as the door to the chamber opened and the man stood beside her, looking out. Mercy shallowed her breath, keeping the smells of pipe tobacco and warm flesh at bay, and gestured towards the garden. She saw his mouth open and close, chattering at her.

'Pepper,' she said, somewhere between a shout and a whisper she hoped. 'Pepper plant, they call it. For the itch.' She mimed scratching at her wrists and fingers. He remembered then, turning to face her, so that she could watch his lips.

'Daphne,' he said and 'Daph-ne,' again. 'Let me write it for you.'

She smiled: that this man – so learned, though not much more than a boy – should know so little of the world beyond his study. He pulled her by the wrist towards the desk, as if she were a child, and made some marks on a piece of paper. She nodded.

'Daphne,' he repeated.

Mercy stared at the dark shapes until he put a finger on her chin, turning her face towards his. 'There is a story —' she watched his lips — 'that Daphne, a beautiful woman, was turned into a tree ...' She lost the rest of the explanation, marked only the warning: 'Take care. It is poisonous.' Mercy nodded again. Already he was back to his books. She collected the sack of laundry and bumped it down the stairs, smiling as she went.

An Education

One morning, early in the year: in the new Botanic Garden, a group of students surrounds a speaker as he (of course he) spins a tale of species identification. All are oblivious to the slight figure standing beside a tree. If one chances to glance in her direction, he will see only a drab garment of coarse cloth partly hidden by a pinafore of even drabber brown, and perhaps a hood which obscures the face. Beside the form, a bundle on the ground. If anyone thought to speculate, he would assume that the woman (of course a woman) was of the servant class, and the burden — laundry? garden waste? — merely set down to rest for a moment. Who would imagine ears which strained to hear, a mind which grappled with the intricacies of the speaker's story, looking for the kernel of knowledge at its heart? And when the students have dispersed and the speaker is walking back to college, he may turn once or twice, puzzled by the shadowy figure following a dozen paces behind. But one such female is much like another, after all.

Darkness settled as she neared the Borough and dragged the washing down the basement steps. No sign of the girl yet. Mercy wondered, not for the first time, whether she might be trying her luck with the maltsters, loitering at the door of the Three Tuns and offering the little she had in exchange for coppers. She shrugged. The fire was almost dead but a faint glow at the base was enough: a few twigs and a handful of pine cones and it was coaxed back to life. She added a faggot from the dwindling pile: she would collect more tomorrow. While the water heated, she felt in her bag for the spray of flowers she had pulled from the bush in the college garden. Held close, though not close enough to start the rash on the skin, she saw that the blossom was composed of stars, four petals with an orange centre. And the scent! Mercy laid the stem on the ledge in front of the slate and rubbed her hands on her apron. The berries were the most potent part, she knew, but adding the crushed petals to hog's lard would make an ointment fragrant enough to persuade the user of its soothing qualities – until it was too late.

A Remedy

The first occasion: mischief only, although God knows she will have reason enough in time. A fine morning, the start of spring. Hedges bud. The leafless branches of the blackthorn are awash with froth, the air loud with birdsong, but there is winter still in the wind. He has been out in all weathers setting the traps, hanging the moles along the wire, and his hands have borne the brunt of it, weeping wounds slow to scab, the knuckles and joints swollen and blistered. He is like a baby with the colic, holding his hands to the fire then screaming with pain. So, she is out early, searching for shoots of chamomile. No flowers yet, but the stems and leaves make a balm which she mixes with pig fat and gentles onto his skin. Sometimes as she takes the reddened paw he recoils, whipping his hand away and landing a clout on the side of her head or across her mouth. The day he makes her nose

bleed is the day she picks a handful of wild daffodils from
the long grass by the river and squeezes the sap into the
ointment. The more the sores worsen, the louder he cries
for comfort, the softer her voice as she applies the cruel
salve. She keeps the daffodils in a jar on the table, smiling
occasionally at their innocently nodding faces.

The next morning the man's chair was empty, coals dead
in the grate. She inhaled the signs: an odour of fennel and
vinegar that spoke of some patent medicine, all expense with
little effect, and an underlying sourness. She knocked on the
door to the inner chamber and pushed it open. He lay in a
swelter of blankets, face flushed, his body contorted with
coughing. He shook his head, closing his eyes when she asked
if he wanted for anything. Still, she cleared and lit the fire and
heated a pan of water, some for a weak tea that she left by the
bed, the rest in the jug by the washstand. Later, she returned
with a sheet washed, a hint of rosemary in its folds, and a syrup
of coltsfoot for his chest, which he took obediently like a baby.
She also brought a small flask of pine oil infused with thyme:
a few drops in a basin of hot water would freshen the air and
help his breathing. She gathered up the damp bedding and sat
for a while, watching as he slept.

In the weeks that followed, her days found a new rhythm.
Waking early, she would tend to the plants outside the entry,
eking out the splash of rusty rainwater from the tin, checking
for caterpillars or blight. A child's windmill rescued from the
gutter kept the birds off. And after the first flurry of curiosity,
the other women were happy to disregard this activity as
another of Mercy's mysteries. Which was just as well, given the
coming harvest.

Later, she walked to the college, dawdling through the
gardens where familiarity made her invisible, collecting a stray

branch or a flower stem as she passed. Her patient was slow to recover but anxious to be back at his books, so she carried the heavy volumes through to the chamber and sat with the man as he read. Sometimes he would read aloud and, though she heard nothing, she would watch his lips move and try to follow the words.

A Sermon

Mercy sits with her husband on a bench at the back of the church, hands in her lap. His eyes are closed, his breathing even. Mercy holds herself still. Although newly married, already she fears the punishment that waits for her at home if she disturbs him. Around them, other families who have gathered out of duty or fear as they have done, trailing the long miles from the huts in the fen to the church on the hill. In front, the wealthy of the parish, with fine clothes and full bellies and pews of their own to sit in. Beyond them and raised up out of reach, the minister in the pulpit has a story to tell. They have prayed and sung, sung and prayed; now they must listen. It's a true story about an expedition which set sail from the River Thames to explore the frozen north and was never seen again. Mercy has heard the tale before, the perils of inviting the wrath of a vengeful god, she supposes. 'Two stout ships and more than a hundred men,' the minister says, 'vanished without trace. Now, one of the greatest artists alive today has painted a picture of what we might see if we could travel so far: icebergs and polar bears, a broken mast with a torn sail, the bones of the dead.' And the title of this painting? The minister scans the upturned faces as if they might have the answer. 'Man proposes, god disposes.'

In May, as the days lengthened, Mercy spent longer in the rooms at the top of the brick stair. Although the man's health was improved, he remained weak, and classes that might have taken place outside were conducted here, the young men eager as puppies to please their master. At first, she avoided these sessions, fearing she would be an encumbrance. Soon, though, she found she could pass unnoticed if she was quiet or busied herself with boiling water or making tea. One afternoon she remained still, seated in the corner between two shelves of books, as the students argued over the identification of a flower – specimens, they called them – watching their lips as they batted the names back and forth. Eventually, their lesson over, they gathered up their books. Closing the door behind them, the man turned towards her.

'And you, Mercy, what do you think?'

Unsure if she had read the words right, she watched his lips for the question a second time.

'What can you tell us about this plant?' He placed the small yellow flower with its leafy stars in her lap.

She looked for mockery in his face and found none. Still, she felt the flush redden her cheeks. 'It is sunkfield.'

He cupped a hand round his ear. 'Louder.'

'It is named sunkfield, or five fingers. Look.' She separated the five toothed leaflets into a fan. 'It is a flower for the fifth month. And it has five hearts.' Mercy pointed to the petals. 'Those who know no better say it will make a young man love. If you hang it by your door, it will keep off witches. And five fingers, one for each sense.' She touched her eyes, the tip of her nose. 'For me, only four.' She placed her hands over her ears, and then pinched off one of the fingers of leaf.

He smiled and said, 'Cinquefoil means five leaves. Its Latin name is *Potentilla* – Little Powerful One.'

Mercy nodded. 'It is strong. It has many powers. Not only the magic. It can cure toothache, the gout and fever, or bruises and swellings. There is another −' She shook her head: how to describe the bush with the purple flowers that grew in the marshy ground on the edge of Coe Fen? 'It stands upright, taller.' She held a hand, palm down, just below her knee, and sketched the line of a long stem in the stuff of her skirt.

He pulled a second chair up to the desk and gestured for her to sit, tugging her by the arm when she shook her head, and set a pencil and a page torn from his notebook in front of her. As she stared at the empty page, the burning in her cheeks began again. Holding the pencil as if it were the knife she used for slicing roots, she made a line that scored right through the paper to the wood beneath. She rubbed at the scratch with a finger, fearing his displeasure. When he merely smiled again, she put aside the pencil and fetched instead a piece of burnt wood from the fireplace. She made the rough mark of a vertical curved at its tip, shorter curves for the fingers of the leaf, some crosses for the toothed edge. As for the flower itself − she shrugged: impossible. He brought a book to the table then and turned the pages, one plant after another appearing like a conjuring trick.

'This?' he said, pointing. She shook her head. 'Or this?' Again no. Eventually, yes, this one. The crimson stars with the spiked suns at their centre blossomed before her eyes. She touched a thumb on the edge of a painted petal, felt the weight of his hand on her forearm and turned to face him, sure now of a reprimand.

'The same family. But how did you know?' he said.

'Family,' Mercy said. 'It is the same. Different, but also the same.'

A Cure for Constipation

She has left him in the hut: he has business to attend to, he says, as he pulls the blanket up around his ears. No doubt he will rise eventually, pull on what he calls his work clothes, swear at the empty pantry and again at the pain in his gut which no amount of straining and swearing in the privy at the end of the yard will ease. She imagines his face bloated with sleep and suspicion of what the world has in store for this day. Perhaps he will try again at the mill or see if he can sell his services to catch rabbits or moles.

Mercy walks out across the fen towards Seven Acre Wood in search of wild greens and something which will ease the congestion in his belly. The snowdrops are finished. There are patches of the yellow stars called pilewort and a mat of stitchwort under the hazel on the edge of the wood. She gathers the leaves and tops without crushing them and lays them in the bottom of the burlap bag. Any that are bruised will do for poultices and ointments; the rest they will eat with the few potatoes left in the sack, along with whatever else they find. No pigweed, but a spread of lamb's quarter in the marshy ground near the river. She crouches by the carpet of boggard's posy: no flowers yet, but they will do. A small bunch goes into her apron pocket, the leaves and stems to prepare a lotion for sore eyes, and the whole plant to be boiled to soothe blains and hives. For the obstruction in his bowel, she adds a further handful and then another, fearing already the malevolence with which he will greet her when she returns home. She runs her hands through the water at the river's edge and wipes them on her skirts.

Late afternoon sun fell across the piles of books and papers, on the side of her face and on the back of the man's hand where it held open the book on which he was working. Mercy watched the veins ripple beneath the skin, felt his presence beside her, close enough for her to reach out and touch his elbow if she so wished. The second chair remained beside his at the table and he took without comment the stems of celandine she had brought. When her work was finished, he showed her the place he had made for her at the desk: paper, a pencil and some pieces of charcoal bought from somewhere in the town – certainly not pulled from the hearth. Her face burnt and burnt more when she saw that her plant was there too, arranged so that the yellow flowers lay clear of the spread of leaf and stem. Beside the plant, a book lay open at its image. She shook her head – too much – but the man frowned, turned on his heel, walked into the chamber and closed the door after him. So she sat, anxious not to displease him further.

Her first attempts on two sides of the paper were a mess of dark smudges and crossed lines. When he returned to his desk, she put these aside and reached for a clean page, glancing in his direction for permission. He spoke, then, pointing at the book, at the marks below the picture. She shook her head. He spelt out the name again, enunciating each segment slowly, '*Chel-i-don-i-um.*'

'Too long!' she said.

He smiled and pointed again to the page. '*Ma-jus* – it means May, flowering in May. Look.' He took her hand, withdrawing his instantly when she flinched as if scalded. Then, guiding her fingers, he traced a zigzag shape on the page, rise and fall, rise and fall. 'Em,' he said. 'Mu – mu – mu. The letter M. For May. And *majus*.'

Mercy ran her fingers along the painted edge of the flower. 'We call it wartweed,' she said. She broke off the end of the stalk and pointed to the liquid that oozed from the stem. 'Rub it on the skin and a wart will be gone. It heals ulcers and sores and all manner of ailments. For the mother.' Mercy rubbed her hands over her belly, touched her breast. 'Or a gargle against the toothache.'

He smiled. 'Its botanical name –' he hesitated on 'botanical', waiting for her nod – 'means swallow, perhaps because it flowers in the month when the swallows arrive. The story says that the mother swallow drops it into the eyes of the young birds to restore their sight.'

Mercy dipped her head in agreement. 'An ointment for sore eyes, to cleanse and clear the sight. A pity it does not work the same magic for the ears.' Mercy covered her ears with her hands so that, if she had to rely on hearing alone, she would have missed his reply.

'It is a poison, too, of course.'

The sun was gone. Darkness thickened in the corners of the room. Mercy stood to leave, pausing for a moment at the desk. With her fingers she traced the shape, the double swoop and dip of the letter, on her blank page. 'It is mu,' she said. 'For May. And for Mercy.'

The Wrath of God

She waits until darkness falls and the last flickers of light in nearby dwellings are extinguished. In the scrub at the back of the hut, she hacks at the weedy ground with the blade of the shovel. Smells of wild garlic and mint fill her head. She sees no one; only once feels a sudden vibration and a frenzy of heat and hooves, the wrath of God become a four-legged fiend as a rider passes the dwelling at a scorching speed and is gone, leaving only the stink of horse behind. She drags the lifeless body to the shallow bed she has hollowed out of the ground and sets it down, before scraping over the mound of displaced earth.

When the body is covered and the earth flattened, she stares into the night, marking a fallen trunk, a hummock of bramble, seeking to fasten the spot in her memory. She picks up the shovel and moves off through the trees. She has work to do at home, packing her meagre possessions, the sleeping draught he took nightly for his bloated gut, the decoction of monkshood in a stoppered bottle inside an old shoe.

She pictures the ruddy face, brutish even in sleep, lips agape with snoring. How easy it had been to remove the cork and allow the liquid to drip into his open mouth.

Mercy pressed the earth round the last of the comfrey seedlings and made a start on the henbane, selecting the strongest and planting them in the shelter of the wall. Then she chose a stem of columbine to take with her, along with a bryony root that she had saved, and the first of the lily of the valley that they call May bells.

'Mu for May. Mu for Mercy.' She had found little enough mercy in her life, she thought: no merciful husband or father in this world, and she saw no reason to believe that the next would be kinder.

As she entered the college gates, the sun warm on her back, a tree with hanging yellow blossoms kicked up its skirts in the breeze. Mercy knew the flower: once, years ago, she had added a few of the seeds to her collection, subscribing to the common belief in their potency. She knew better now: it was good enough to unsettle the stomach, or to inflict the vulnerable with convulsions, but something stronger was needed to be sure of a speedy death. Now a wall dripped with foamy violet clusters, clearly cousins of the yellow blossoms. Mercy breathed deep, savouring their scent. And here another blast of perfume: under the great chestnut, a patch of bluebells. The strip of woodland out towards Madingley was a fragrant ocean at this time of year. She would walk there tomorrow, collect a clump or two of the bulbs, like enough to the onion to escape the attention of the careless or the unsuspecting as a useful addition to a final supper and a flower to take to the college the following day. Already she felt the unaccustomed weight of the pencil in her fingers and saw the curve of the bell emerging in the marks she would make on the page.

FLOWERS

EMMA TIMPANY

This is the place: four fields in the shape of a rough parallelogram. On her left, one part of the closest field is enclosed behind wire mesh. A path runs through long, wet grass towards a gate in the fence. Ahead of her is an open-fronted barn with a caravan parked inside it, a chimney rising from its roof.

She cannot see anyone. She is about to leave when, looking again, she notices a figure kneeling inside the fencing.

She walks over but he does not seem to know she is there. He wears a suit, some kind of woollen weave, not tweed.

'Hello.'

'Hello.'

He is young, younger than her. He stands and wipes his hands on his clothes. His hair is flat and yellowish. Despite his smile, his face is the wrong kind of white. He has been ill. Is still ill, perhaps.

'Rachel said you wanted someone to grow flowers.'

'Yes.' He shakes his head as if confused. 'I only just woke up. I still have to sleep a lot. But I remember now.'

She doesn't know what to say. She doesn't know what she was expecting but it was not this.

'Are you cold?' he says. 'It's cold today.'

And bleak, she does not say, this place is bleak.

'Let's have some tea.'

The barn smells of dirt and straw, the caravan of damp. His bed is a heap of sleeping bags and blankets; the cups are stained with a thick layer of tannin. Roll-up butts huddle, crushed together in a jar lid.

'Sit down. Here.' He moves a pile of books from a seat. 'Rachel said you were a florist.'

'Well, yes. Sort of. I never meant to be. It wasn't what I wanted.'

He lights the camp stove, rolls a cigarette.

'My family were. Florists, I mean. My grandfather lost his job in the Great Depression. Five kids and nothing to eat. So my grandmother started growing flowers.' She doesn't know why she is telling him this. She doesn't tell anyone this. She shakes her head.

'I don't have any biscuits.'

'It doesn't matter.'

'I only have goat's milk. Is that okay?'

'Yes.' She has never drunk goat's milk. 'That's okay.'

It is raining. In her mind the earth has a red tint but now she sees that, under the rain, the soil is deep brown, black, almost. He has laid out some beds within the wire mesh, six rectangles of soil. The fence is to keep out the rabbits which will otherwise eat everything.

'Look.' He points to a line of feathery green leaves. 'I planted them in December and they're up already.'

'Are they a type that grows in winter?'

'No. I was late putting them in because I was in hospital. All this should have been done earlier, in the autumn. This soil must be good soil.'

It looks like good soil but she will not know until she starts to work it. The rain is heavy now, too heavy for her to begin.

In the shelter of the barn, he shows her rows of tools. Most are old but some are new, their dull, silver light an oddity among the rest, the well-used and the worn.

The next time, there is no sign of him, though she scans the field for a crouched figure in a suit. Inside the barn, still air that could mistakenly be called warm but is only the cessation of wind. Through the caravan window, she sees him curled up on his side, blankets heaped around him, holes in the bottom of his socks.

She climbs over the rabbit fence and puts a bin bag, filled with bags of bulbs and packets of seeds, down by the side of the bed of freshly dug earth he indicated, last time, that she could plant. Returns to the barn for tools along the path of beaten grass. Begins to mark out a row.

The rows of vegetables in the neighbouring beds are all perfectly straight. By contrast, the trench she has made wavers. She goes back to her row and tries to even it up, mentally making a list of the things she will need – bamboo poles, string.

The soil smells slightly of iron, of leaves. Small stones appear occasionally but the earth has a lightness to it. She opens a packet of bulbs – tulips – and looks at them in the dim light. It is three months past the optimum time to plant them. She bought them cheaply from a local discount store but they look in good condition, a bright brown, shiny sheath on the outside of the pure white bulb. Plant at twice the depth of bulb. She lays them out fifteen centimetres apart then covers them.

The beds are larger than she thought. She adds sawdust to the list in her head. The last seeds she plants are poppies. Light, tiny, they are indistinguishable from the soil as soon as she sows them.

'You've been busy.' He is wearing an old oilskin over his suit.
'Yes.'

'What have you been planting?'

'Bulbs', she says. 'Seeds.' She fumbles for the packets and hands them to him. Her jeans are soaked from where she has been kneeling.

'These are nice.' He holds the empty poppy packet.

'They were free. I wouldn't have bought them. Because the flowers only last a day or so. Still, I can use the seed heads.'

'That's a shame. About the flowers.'

'It's often the way. The most beautiful don't last.'

He is looking at her rows.

'I should have made them straight. Next time I'll bring some string.'

'I've got some. Poles and string. Didn't you see them in the barn?'

'No.'

Before he got ill, he tells her, he was a set designer. Now he works on the field. The quiet here, the growing things. It is his way of making himself better.

'Look, peregrine.'

She does not want to look but, raising her head, she follows his finger to where the bird flies through veils of rain.

'We should go in. Shelter from this. Do you want tea?'

'No, thanks. I'm soaked.' She is cold now, having been still for so long. The thought of sitting in the caravan is not a pleasant one. 'I'll be back next week.'

She knocks mud off the spade and fork and carries them back to the barn. He opens the caravan door; warmth from the camp stove drifts out. Condensation fogs the windows. He is smiling at her, and she wonders what he is going to say.

'Could you bring some milk when you come next time? I can't have dairy. Goat's milk. Or soya.'

'Sure,' she says.

Back at the car she takes off her gumboots, her soaking coat, and loads them into the boot. Strips off her jeans and wraps her lower half in a blanket. Drives home that way.

From the highest point, where she now stands, and the high point opposite her, the land creases down, as if it has been folded on the diagonal, into the corner farthest from her. Because he is working near the bottom of the crease, it is hard to make out what he is doing.

She has forgotten the milk.

It has already started to bother her that it is his soil, his earth, his rules. That she is merely scratching, borrowing a few centimetres of surface. And yet she cannot imagine belonging to this place, it being hers. It is not what she would choose for herself. It is too high, too exposed. The jumbled boulders of the carn seem, at times, a reflection of her confusion. And then there is the cold, a deep earth-and-stone cold, the kind that gets in your bones. She wonders again what is wrong with him, what was wrong with him.

The quiet, though, also has a way of its own. In the way her life is away from this place, it feels like nourishment. Every action she initiates proceeds, unthwarted, until it is complete. No one else to consider except for the too-thin man she sees out of the corner of her eye.

She is planting *Liatris spicata*. The bulbs are dark, knobbly, a light hair of old, dried roots on their bases. Their hairiness reminds her of sea potatoes, found on the nearby beaches at low tide. When she looks up she notices two parallel rows of bamboo canes, joined at their apex, stand in one of the beds. Supports for beans, perhaps, or peas. Everything he does out here, in the beds, is so neat. But it is not neat in the barn or in the caravan.

No rain today but it is cold. Smoky-yellow light crouches at the edges of the sky. Next, she plants a row of *Camassia leichtlinii*, a cultivar of quamash. The bulbs are white and smooth, small green shoots already sprouting from their apical points. It is far too late to be planting them. She tries to think of May, when these bulbs will produce long, straight, green stems, and then star-shaped flowers, blue and cream.

She hears the soft sound of his boots on the grass. As she turns, reluctant to stop her work, she briefly wonders what he thinks of her. Her neck aches, so she rubs it.

'More bulbs.'

'Yes. Look at these.' She lifts an *Eremurus stenophyllus* tuber from brown paper, holding towards him the flat disc with leggy roots, like the dried limbs of a once fleshy spider.

'And they'll stay in the soil? Or will you lift them?'

'No. They'll stay. They form clumps. Bulbs like these, perennials, reproduce themselves asexually. Clone themselves, basically. So you get more flowers year on year.'

This seems to surprise him. She has no idea what he knows or doesn't know about flowers.

The next time there are lots of people at the field. It takes her a while to find him. People talk to her, seem interested in what she is doing. They tell her things about the man who owns the field, assuming she knows more than she does. Without her prompting, his secrets spill out on the grass. They all seem excited by the fact that their friend has this surfeit of space. Many of them live on boats, in vans and caravans squeezed into corners of fields or the fringes of towns and villages.

She sees him in the distance, reassesses his age down a notch and then down again. How aged he is by illness, by the experience of illness. It makes him more like her; it is the bridge that links her on one side and his friends on the other.

She has found out, quite recently, that her brother has been lying to her. For years, he has stolen from her, from the joint assets left to them by their parents. He calls what he did an act of love. It is not love. There is a chance that she will lose her house, lose everything she has worked for.

The friends start dragging dead wood into a circle. Someone sets light to it. Bottles appear and a keg of beer. She plants *Nectaroscordum siculum*, an onion-paper fine sheath over its bulbs, which will one day be a handful of purple-and-green-striped bells dangling from a wiggly stem. By the time she finishes, darkness is come. She looks over to the circle of light. The flames give his face the colour it normally lacks. She catches a glimpse of how he must have looked and how he might, perhaps, look again one day.

In the weak sunlight, the green tips of the first bulbs she planted poke through the earth, cast tiny purple shadows on the soil, and she sees what he has described to her but she has never really believed. There is a view of the sea. Distant, complex with lines of trees and land in the foreground and further back a skewed triangle of mint green water, a violet horizon.

Tomorrow, February tips into March. In the soil she finds a lime green grub, curled and sleeping. More seeds have broken through the earth; tiny as watercress, they tremble as if exhausted by the division of their first leaf into two. In the hearts of the hyacinths, flower spikes push upwards.

She knocks on the caravan door. No reply. She opens it, pulls a pint of goat's milk from her pocket, leaving it on the floor where she hopes he will see it.

The goat's milk was fresh today 28/2. See you next week?

She is annoyed that she brought him milk and he isn't here. But she is also pleased. Words have stopped, are trapped inside her. She does not want to talk. She wants to plant flowers, rows and rows of flowers, and wait and watch and tend them as they grow.

'Thank you for the milk.'

'I didn't bring any today.'

'What are you planting?'

'Lavender.' She has bought plug plants and potted them on, hardened them off in her courtyard garden; against the vastness of the field, they seem tiny. She plants them through a layer of weed matting, cutting crosses and slotting one plant into each gap.

'How long will they last for?'

'They'll grow and get bigger for about ten years or so. And then they'll die off.'

As the day ends, she hears the sound of cars, footsteps and voices echoing down the track, the clink of bottles. The friends build a fire with new, dry boughs. They distract him, keep him busy talking. In the fading light, he shifts from old to young, young to old.

Her back aches. She tidies her things and looks at what she has achieved. There is little to see; the bulk of her labour lies beneath the surface of the soil.

The sky is a serious blue, which means that darkness is not far away. Through the still air she hears the sharp crackle of flames and smells dry wood burning.

Today she plants the last of the bulbs, some alliums, the *Triteleia laxa*, and the sweet pea seeds, pre-scored. The poppies and the cornflowers are through. The love-lies-bleeding. The soil is warming. The irises have produced grey, strap-fine leaves. A violet ground beetle scuttles away under her hand. An idea, a question, a friend of a friend – all of these things have led her here. Now, the hyacinths are opening. As she cuts through their thick, sappy stems, washes the dirt off the leaves and lower flowers, the few open bells release a clean, sweet scent.

He has also been planning and planting. She has helped him to lift off turf and peel it back in preparation for a second row of beds.

The weeds have started to grow; the perennial buttercup, its net-like roots spread horizontally, is particularly hard to shift. She tracks the white roots of dandelions, zigzags of light in the dark soil, their wounds leaking a milky sap.

He digs for a while and then he stops and coughs. Whatever is wrong with him is taking its time to give up its hold.

He has gone to drink water, hand resting on the tap until the coughing eases. His clothes still hang on him like the clothes on a scarecrow. When was he last well? When did he last live in a house? She considers this coldness, rising from the earth, his enemy. She thinks he does not do enough to protect himself against it. How can he become better if he is not warm?

How will he get better if he drinks from filthy mugs?

He has seen her looking at him and now he beckons her. She climbs over the fence, her shoulders tense.

He points to a new ridge of earth by the side of the barn. From here she can see thin sticks are planted in it.

'Willows,' he says.

'They'll grow big.'

'I know.'

'Why here?'

'Because this is where the house will go.'

'You're building a house?'

'One day.'

'To live in?'

'Isn't that why most people build houses?'

'I thought …' But she doesn't know what she had thought.

He begins talking about dwelling rights, planning permission. The house will be built out of straw bales with wool as insulation.

She cuts the *Camassia leichtlinii 'Alba'*, secures five stems with a rubber band and drops them in a bucket. The alliums are ready, tall Gladiator and the squat lavender starburst of *Allium christophii*. Once they are all cut and bunched, she moves them into the shade. Dahlia tubers lie in the trench. She covers them with soil, then plants sedum around the edges of the bed, a type with purple-black leaves and, come September, small, hard, ruby flowers.

She is beginning to realise that he did not think she would plant anything permanent. He expected that she would grow flowers from seed and harvest them, an annual crop. There has been this miscommunication right from the beginning, probably the result of her reluctance to talk, his assumption that flowers were grown in the same way as vegetables.

She tells herself it does not matter. Everything she plants, with a couple of exceptions, can be dug up again and moved. Like people, flowers travel: transplanted with care, they usually manage to re-establish themselves, to put down new roots.

Twice in her life she has tried to run away from flowers, the first time from her family's floristry business, the second time when, out of necessity, she worked as a florist in London. Yet here she is, back among them. They follow her, it seems. Or she, unwittingly, unwillingly, follows them. They present themselves to her as opportunities, the only options.

She knows their common and Latin names. Some have been her companions since earliest childhood, their names learnt alongside her own; they have always been among the most important inhabitants of her world. The flowers she grows, that line up wonkily behind her back like a beautiful army, are not as delicate as they look. They are survivors.

She is ready to go. She walks over to where he is working, beside the willow bank.

'Goodbye,' she says.

'I'm going to get a digger in, to grade the earth flat for the house,' he says. 'I'll get them to scoop out a pond while they're here.'

'I brought you some milk,' she says.

'Come and see the pond,' he says.

A shallow basin has been scraped out below the flower beds, the excess soil tipped at the southerly edge, building it up into a bank; the effect is pleasing, as if the far lip of the pond were somehow floating above the lower parts of the field.

In her childhood garden, there was a stream dividing the formal beds around the house from the secret spaces of a stand of native bush. A simple bridge, arch-backed, connected the two worlds. She remembers what it was to paddle in that stream, the little beach of pale gold gravel it left before it exited the property, edged by a rustling screen of bamboo.

So water, yes.

Nothing exists without water.

So many things are flowering: *Liatris spicata*, *Eryngium planum*, nigella, cornflowers, sweet peas. She comes early to cut the flowers, weeds a little, covers the soil in mulch to stop it losing moisture to the sun and is ready to leave by midday.

When she hears the caravan door open she looks up, expecting to see him, but a woman emerges and walks towards the standpipe to fill the kettle.

'Hello.'

'Who are you?' the woman says.

'I'm the one who grows the flowers.'

He comes out of the caravan, rubbing his hair.

'When you're finished, can you give Jo a lift back to town?' he says. 'Are you finished?'

'Yes. Pretty much. Just tidying up.'

'We haven't had breakfast yet,' Jo says. 'We haven't even had a cup of tea.'

'You can have breakfast when you get home.'

'Are you trying to get rid of me,' Jo says, 'before I've had a cup of tea?'

'Of course not,' he says. 'I'll make you some tea.' He turns to where she is standing between the flowerbeds. 'Would you like tea too?'

'No, thanks,' she says. 'I'm going soon. But I brought some milk.'

As she carries the flowers to the edge of the track, Jo sits on one of the benches by the fire circle and talks to her. The things Jo says are funny in a pithy kind of way. She's pretty, too.

He brings out two mugs of tea.

'I'm off now.'

'Do you mind giving Jo a lift?'

'Not at all.'

'I think I'll spend the day here,' Jo says, stretching and looking around. 'It's going to be a beautiful day.'

'Do what you like,' he says. 'But you should know I've got work to do.'

'Don't mind me.' Jo lies back on the boards, folding her hands over her ribs, shutting her eyes. 'I'll be just fine.'

The pond water is pale bronze, the suspended particles of soil in it yet to settle. He is wading, thigh deep, forearms immersed, planting marginals below the surface. The scent of water is softly mineral, a note of freshness amongst the dry grass and the dust.

Flower buds form on the tiny lavender bushes; the leaves of the sedum are dark as wine. What is winter? Its memory lies in the earth, beneath the bark of the shrubs, the trees. It lies in leaves that tremble in the light. It lies in pollen, gold and grey, which the bees collect and carry with them from flower to flower.

When she looks over to the pond again she sees him floating on his back, arms and legs splayed out, five-pointed as a fallen star.

Years later, on the day she comes to dig up the last of the flowers, he is not there. He has gone to work in Greece for a while, Jo tells her. On a sustainable building project.

Jo stands in the doorway of the house made of straw. 'I've got a flat in a proper house again,' she says. 'I'm moving on, too.'

The wool they'd used as insulation had been full of moth larvae. They'd had a massive infestation, as well as trouble with mice.

'What sort of trouble with mice?'

'They were falling out of the ceiling onto my face,' Jo says, 'while I was asleep.'

'What can be done?'

Jo shrugs. Perhaps the moths have got into the straw. Perhaps the house will have to be torn down, and they'll start again somehow. He's gone away to have time to think things through.

Time to think. She had had it, in the hours that she spent here on her knees, eyes on the ground, hands in the good earth.

The willows he grew from sticks reach above her head. The lavenders have filled out from tiny plugs to dense, thick pads. They will remain, along with some other plants that are difficult to shift. Though she tries to lift them carefully, she is bound to miss some bulbs. After she is gone, they will put up their heads each spring, aiming for the light.

Will he think of them as a nuisance?

Or a gift?

Five years on she has managed to reclaim most of what was lost. Now she is moving to a new house with a garden big enough to hold all these flowers.

Time to say goodbye.

She walks over to the pond. On its green-grey surface water lilies float, white and cream and copper-red, stands of sedge and flag iris softening its edges, and she feels it, as she felt it when she was a child, flowers all around her: a sense of dissolution between here and now and whatever lies just out of reach.

Here.

All that has filtered down into the darkness has given life to flowers that open like a hand; in the centre of each a deepening of colour, which she can hear as if it were a sound.

Nothing exists without water.

She thinks of him and knows that he is well.

THE GARDEN OF THE NON-COMPLETER FINISHER

ANGELA SHERLOCK

In the middle of the village there's a duck pond, which is as it should be. It comes to the road on this side, but over there a nice grassy bank slopes down to the water and that's where the children come to throw bread for the birds. There's a weeping willow, which, again, is an appropriate adornment, and of course masses of daffodils in the spring.

Tourists, driving through on their way to somewhere else, will stop to take photographs. The ducks are used to this and pose obligingly, but parking is a problem, and a queue of cars builds up, tooting impatiently, in a hurry to get some where important.

I didn't mention the pub. There is one, of course, the something Arms, named after the Lord of the Manor's family, long extinct and some of them stretched out in stone in the church. So we've got a pond, a pub, a church. We need something else. It ought to be market day or perhaps a summer fete, to complete the picture. And we are in luck, for it is Open Gardens Day. This is a great opportunity to have a nose around places usually closed to us, to pass judgement on each other, to see who is the best.

Let's meet the judges first. There are three of them – Roger Morley, who likes to think of himself as the local squire; Gillian Beaumont, who runs everything and enjoys meddling; and the vicar. He's coming close to retirement and his wife is worrying about how they will manage downsizing from the spacious vicarage.

I'll stop talking now and we can follow them as they march through the village, Gillian with her notebook, Roger with his Dictaphone, and the vicar who nods amiably at everyone they meet.

This is Marjorie Tilling's house. A natural hedge, hawthorn, blackthorn and such, protects her garden from prying eyes. The front is flagged, pots and tubs, an arrangement of garden furniture, and Harry's built-in barbecue. This is not what we have come to see. Our judges wend their way down the path and through the side gate, which swings open to reveal the circle of lawn fringed with dahlias, red hot pokers, golden rod, gladioli, all arranged according to height and glowing in the sunlight. Roger digs in his pocket, extracts his phone, and takes pictures from several angles. Gillian is jotting down her comments and frowns as Roger murmurs into his Dictaphone. Marjorie is in the window. She peers through the leaded panes, a little nervous, but contestants are not allowed to speak to the judges so she tries not to catch anyone's eye. She remembers, with a little flare of hope, that Gillian seemed very grateful last week when she had given her a lift into Teignbury to collect her Land Rover from the garage.

Gillian had talked at Marjorie all the way, criticising everyone on the parish council, complaining about the changes to postal delivery times, which meant that she got her letters later.

'And the *London Review of Books*, Marjorie. I do think they should stop giving that Mantel woman a platform for her anti-royalty rants. Alan Bennett, now, such a treasure.'

Marjorie does not read the *London Review of Books* but she has read Bennett's *The Uncommon Reader* and thought that perhaps Gillian hadn't. And she smiled to herself at the thought of *Smut*. She still felt rather guilty at having enjoyed that, and she hadn't told Harry about it. He might have thought it was pornographic. The vicar gives her a little wave as they turn to leave and Marjorie sighs. It would be lovely to win, but, as Harry would say, that is not a very realistic prospect. She goes through to the kitchen and puts the kettle on. It's too early for a gin and tonic.

'Very bright, wasn't it?' This is Roger. 'Clashed a bit, I thought.'

Gillian wrinkles her nose.

'Poor Marjorie. She does try. I think she's after a hot look, sort of South African.'

She has never been to South Africa, but has seen enough botanical gardens and seed catalogues to recognise the effect for which Marjorie strives. They circle the pond, heading for Gerry Walton's house. This is probably one of the oldest in the village, ancient and timber-framed and venerable. Rather like Gerry, the vicar thinks, as they survey the garden across the stone wall, which froths with tumbles of aubretia and snow-in-summer and ivy-leaved toad flax. Gerry has gone for a series of raised beds. He says this is so that he can change them every year but the reality is that his knees do not bend as they used to. Shrubs and perennials hug the perimeter, and they wear a slightly shorn look, Gerry having panicked that they were untidy and he'd gone at them yesterday evening when the light was fading.

Gillian bends down to sniff the oriental lilies and comes away with a dab of pollen on her nose. Neither of the men will mention this.

'He's tried a bit too hard,' Roger says. The vicar thinks it looks quite nice and reminds them that they need to go through to the back garden. Gerry has left the gate open so that they won't have to speak to him, and has retreated into the conservatory. He did win once, a few years ago now, but it would be nice … He shakes the thought away and takes a bite of his chocolate digestive, not noticing the trail of crumbs that adorns his cardigan.

'Oh, I say, this is rather good.' Roger again, always the first to speak. He is admiring Gerry's vegetable garden, the orderly, leafy rows that march down the beds, the bamboo tepees of climbing beans, and he feels a little jealous.

'But how can he eat it all?' Gillian is momentarily blinded by sunlight glinting off the greenhouse.

'He, um, gives it away, I expect,' says the vicar, who doesn't admit that he is one of the recipients of this bounty. He is eyeing the great trusses of tomatoes that press against the greenhouse windows and realises that he is feeling rather hungry. It would be nice if someone could offer them a cup of tea, perhaps, and one of Gerry's biscuits. But they must get on.

They all admire the hanging baskets outside the pub but it is known that Matthew hires some company to come in to do them.

'Haven't got the time myself, now we've expanded and got the restaurant.'

It's the same in the beer garden, lovely tubs all carefully dead-headed and regularly watered, but not Matthew's doing.

He'd come to the village, oh, three or four years ago now, and they didn't like him at first. The pub had been a bit dusty and worn, and when he remodelled and redecorated, everyone decided that they'd liked it better before, even though most of them rarely went there, which was why the previous couple had to sell up. But the Sunday roasts, vegetarian option available, got popular, then the Tuesday quiz nights and the Thursday curry nights. All fresh local produce, some of it Gerry's, and the money was a useful addition to his pension.

'Have you tried Matthew's wine tasting nights?' Gillian asks the vicar, but Roger answers, saying they're quite good but a bit pricey.

'We like them,' Gillian says. 'And there isn't anywhere else here to get good wines. Have you seen what she stocks in the village shop?'

Yes, the vicar has seen, and that is where his wife gets the occasional bottle of Zinfandel or Liebfraumilch. But even those, on a vicar's stipend, have to be very occasional. His knees are beginning to ache and he wonders if he should get them checked at the doctor's as Eleanor keeps saying. But his sister had a knee replacement and look how wrong that went.

'Who's next?' Roger knows who's next because he's got the list in his hand, but he doesn't like to go too long without having said anything. It's that hippy couple in the little cottage up the lane. Well, they're not really hippies but she wears long skirts and he's got a beard and they've only been here ten years. As he pushes open the gate, the vicar is relieved to see there's a bench under a great overhang of rambling rose, and he goes to sit on it, feeling defiant as Gillian raises an eyebrow at him.

'Is it a Cecile Brunner?' she asks, looking up at the great tangle. Then, 'No, it can't be. Too late in the year. But it's very pretty. Shame there's no scent.'

'And that clematis,' Roger waves at it. 'Gone a bit wild that, could do with chopping back, eh vicar?'

The vicar is watching all the bees in the great bed of lavender, deciding this is his favourite garden – but that could be because of the bench. He looks up at Roger, wishing that sometimes people would call him by his name, not by his job. He suspects that even Eleanor thinks of him as 'Vicar', remembering when she used to whisper, 'Johnny, oh my Johnny', as she nibbled his ear lobe. But that was a long time ago.

'They ought to move the compost heap,' says Gillian. 'It's not very attractive, is it? And neither is that water butt or those wheelie bins. I've got nice woven willow screens around mine. They make them locally and it would be an improvement.' Gillian went on a willow weaving course when she was Lady President of the Women's Institute. She had not been very good at it.

'It all looks organic,' the vicar says. 'Very eco-friendly. And that's important, isn't it? Are we judging on that?'

Gillian and Roger shake their heads emphatically, thinking of the range of artificial fertilisers and pesticides that keep their gardens under control.

'I should think that clematis is a haven for snails, and all the crushed shells in the world won't keep them off it.' She is pointing at the sea shells scattered through the border, then laughs as a snail makes its stately way across them. The vicar thinks that for all her church going she is not a very Christian woman. She is making notes and Roger is taking photos when a dog comes barking down the path and dances around them excitedly. The vicar holds out his hand for the dog to sniff, but it backs away.

'Bloody mongrel,' Roger says as he tries to launch a kick at it, which only sets the dog off yapping louder. A woman appears at the side gate and when the dog ignores her commands she comes up the path to retrieve the miscreant, smiling apologetically as she bends down to grasp his collar. She confides to the dog, 'My lips are sealed, Hector. I'm not allowed to talk to them and you could get me disqualified,' before she turns and hauls the dog back into the house.

Gillian ponders this. 'Does that count? She did speak in front of us.'

Roger thinks that's enough to disqualify her but the vicar holds his ground. 'The rules say must not speak to the judges, not in front of them.'

And Gillian concedes, since they weren't going to win anyway, although she makes a note to amend the rules for next year. The vicar is feeling much better, glad to have made a stand even though he was sitting down at the time. This lifts his spirits even more since he can repeat it to Eleanor, 'taking a stand while sitting down' and perhaps he could slip it into a sermon. He doesn't notice that his opinion of the garden has been overruled before he can even voice it.

The trio gathers in the lane, Roger and Gillian consulting their lists and their notes. Feeling refreshed, and perhaps a little combative, the vicar goes back to the subject of organic gardening.

'It really ought to be one of the criteria, you know, how natural it is, how organic.'

Roger is feeling rather defensive.

'There's nothing unnatural about fertiliser. NPK, nitrogen, phosphorus, potassium. All naturally occurring.'

The vicar tries to bring up the subject of neonicotinoids but Gillian brushes this aside. 'We really need to speed up a bit. We've still got this lot to see,' waving at Roger's lists, 'and we're not halfway through yet.'

The vicar follows them, trying to recall his chemistry lessons. Aren't nitrogen and potassium used in gunpowder?

And phosphorus, wasn't that what they used in the bombing of Dresden? He ponders the double nature of chemicals, their good uses and their bad. Now, how would that fit into a sermon? The good thief on the cross, perhaps, only it's not the right time of the year. He listens to *Thought for the Day* every morning, marvelling at the way they always manage to be so topical, leaping from the morning's headlines to religious dogma, and all in a few minutes. He's coming up for 70 and finding it hard going to convince his parishioners of the relevance of the church. None of the young ones come any more.

'And none of the gardeners are young, are they?'

Gillian turns, surprised, and he realises he has spoken aloud. He smiles, shaking his head, and murmurs an apology. The two ahead pick up their pace and they rattle through the next gardens. He is getting used to trailing along in their wake and begins to think unchristian thoughts about the size of Gillian's bottom and the sound of Roger's voice. They are supposed to be a team, which reminds him of that course he was sent on, all the qualities you need for a team to work and how to get the subdeacons and the lay ministers with the right skills. And what nonsense it had been. Whoever designed those team roles had never worked in a parish. While they are inspecting the Miller garden (why on earth plant a Japanese garden in Sussex?), the vicar muses on the qualities of his fellow judges. Roger would like to think of himself as a shaper, dynamic, full of drive. And Gillian? She'd certainly award herself completer finisher status. And all the rest of them, probably, from creative through to specialist knowledge.

'Very calming, vicar, don't you think? Very Zen.'

'But not terribly British, is it? All this mindfulness stuff.' Roger again, and so loudly that they can probably hear him in the house.

'Buddhism, apparently, has a lot to offer. Or so I've been told. Um, how many more to see?'

He speeds up when Gillian announces that they are coming to the last one.

'That woman who used to work in the farm shop. Little dusty woman, the sort whose name you can never remember.'

Since she has just looked up the name on Roger's list, the vicar concludes that this garden is not going to be a winner.

'It's over there, that high wall with all the wisteria trailing over the top. Honestly, it makes such a mess when it's flowered, bits scattered everywhere.' She turns the page of her notebook. 'But I've never been inside.'

They skirt the war memorial and Roger has to put his shoulder to the door, which drags noisily as it scrapes across the flags. 'Needs lifting,' he pronounces. 'And could do with a coat of paint.'

He startles a flock of sparrows, which fly off in a panic, and a feather floats down to rest on his collar. Gillian is frowning as she surveys the garden. They go up two steps and are confronted by a raised bed rampant with White Molly, an assortment of annuals and perennials poking through it.

'It's … it's very untidy,' Gillian says. 'Well, it's all rather a mess actually. Look at that.' She points indignantly at the border where rudbeckia and geraniums and purple coneflowers tilt out of the bed and ivy claws its way up the stone wall behind. 'And the verbena! It looks as if it's drunk, the way it's bending over.'

Roger joins in. 'She's left all her tools out. Didn't she know we were coming? And there's washing on the line, dammit.' As he turns accusingly towards the rotary line it pirouettes cheerfully and trails some of the washing through a trough of acidanthera.

But the vicar has seen a jug and glasses set out on the wooden table and suddenly realises how thirsty he is. 'She's left us something to drink.' Lifting the pretty beaded muslin cloth he sniffs the jug and declares it homemade lemonade. 'Delicious. Won't you have some?'

He has spilt a drop and a bee comes to inspect it before heading for the comfrey. Roger's ruddy complexion hints at a habit of imbibing something stronger than lemonade and Gillian is incensed, suspecting bribery.

'Why is everything so crooked?' She gestures at the bed where all the flowers, crowded together, lean lopsidedly, falling over each other as if they were making a bid for escape.

The vicar looks up at the sky, squinting in the sunlight. 'It's because of the walls, I think. They're after the sunlight. Oh look, there are three different kinds of butterflies in the verbena.'

'And the bird feeders.' Gillian points at the scattered seeds and husks. 'She hasn't even swept up. Honestly.' She scribbles in her notebook while Roger shakes his head.

'I don't think I need to bother with photographs. Have you seen all the weeds, for heaven's sake! She's even left a heap of them there, on the side. And there's grass growing between the paving stones. Doesn't look nice and I should think it's a trip hazard.'

They consult together, furious at the insult they have been offered. Roger is getting angrier by the minute. She has wasted their time and he's going to bring it up at the next meeting. Such people!

'I thought he was going to say, "they ought not to be allowed"', the vicar tells Eleanor later. 'He got positively incandescent.' They are in their garden, drinking the bottle of Sauvignon Blanc that the committee awarded for taking part in the judging. It goes rather well with cauliflower cheese. The vicar looks out across the lawn, which has not been cut for some time and presents a lot of trip hazards. The euphorbia has run amok in the border and the roses need deadheading. The garden of a non-completer finisher, he decides, just like hers. He smiles as he remembers pouring himself another glass of her lemonade: looking up, he had seen a woman at one of the windows on the first floor. He had raised his glass in salute. And she smiled down on him.

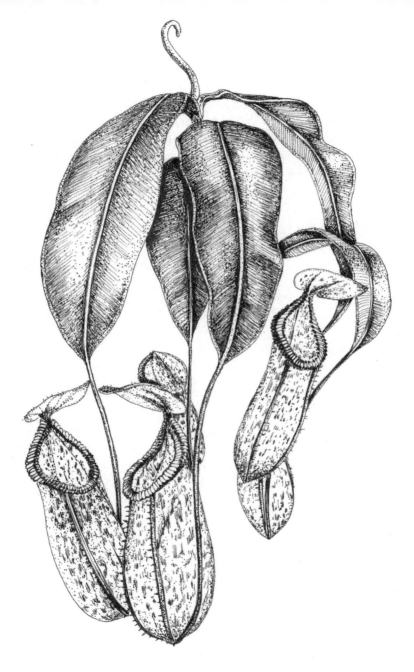

MONKEY CUPS, *Nepenthes*

IN SEARCH OF MONKEY CUPS

HILDEGARD DUMPER

Amanda jumped down from the jeep, pulling at the linen blouse and trousers she was wearing that stuck to her with sweat. What had felt lightweight in M&S on Oxford Street now felt thick and heavy. The heat and humidity were overpowering. Somewhat shell-shocked, she looked around. Only forty-eight hours ago she'd boarded a flight from Heathrow to Singapore, then an overnight train to Kuala Lipis, followed by a bumpy ride by jeep to join a team of fellow botanists.

She was looking down a street of low terraced buildings. On one corner a grocery store, on the other a coffee shop. Just as she was deliberating what to do, a man in jeans and a floral shirt emerged from the coffee shop, his smile warm and friendly. 'You must be Amanda,' he said, offering his hand. 'I'm Hisham, from the Malaysian Botanical Society. Welcome to Malaysia.' And with that he led her inside.

Chairs and tables on a large verandah overlooked a wide, fast-flowing river. Small groups of men sat chatting, while others sat quietly reading newspapers. Hisham led her to a table in the far corner and introduced her. A woman wearing a loose shirt, jeans and headscarf, looking distinctly fed up, was his wife, Faridah. Next to her in a shirt, baggy shorts, and sandals was Cheng, Professor of Botany from the University of Singapore. 'Tea?' Hisham asked, and without waiting for a reply, called for another glass.

The waiter filled their chunky glasses with hot tea and gestured towards a tin of condensed milk with two holes punched on either side. As she poured, the milk dropped straight to the bottom of her glass, forming a dense layer contrasting with the translucent liquid resting above. Fascinated, she picked up a teaspoon and started playing with it, watching the condensed milk swirl through the tea in curls and waves.

Hisham explained they were shortly to travel upriver to their accommodation for the night. Anything they might have forgotten for the journey should be purchased here. This was their last chance, before leaving civilisation. With a few minutes to spare, Amanda made her way to the grocery store. The Chinese shopkeeper, leaning against the doorframe, gave a curt nod and moved aside as she approached. The store was functional and austere, with no shiny, cheap trinkets or brightly coloured sweets to encourage the casual visitor to linger. Shelves were utilitarian, stocked with basic foodstuffs and cleaning products: boxes of Omo and Daz, large round, green tins of the health drink Milo, packets of tea and coffee, chunky, square bars of Sunlight soap, and tins of Bear Brand condensed milk. Flagons of cooking oil and sacks of rice and coffee filled the floorspace. Piles of durians lay in one corner, and long bunches of bananas hung from rafters. Tucked away in the corner she saw a colourful stack of material — sarongs — and pounced on them delightedly. She had always wanted one.

The others were waiting under the shade of a large tree when she came out. Faridah looked critically at the sarong clutched in her arms. 'You could have got a nicer one at KL's Central Market for half the price,' she sniffed.

Faridah was there on sufferance, persuaded by Hisham to accompany him so that Amanda would not be the only female in the group. Having an unmarried woman among a group of males could be embarrassing for them and frowned upon by the people they encountered in the course of the expedition, possibly jeopardising its success. But the jungle was not an environment Faridah had grown up in or had any interest in. Employed as an accountant with a multinational company, she was happiest in the pristine world of Cyberjaya, Malaysia's Silicon Valley, where the natural world was strictly controlled and kept at a safe distance.

They were overlooking a wide confluence of two rivers. Hisham explained that the Pahang River flowed below them, while opposite was the mouth of the Tembeling River. He went on to tell Amanda and Cheng that the Tembeling valley was once a centre of late Neolithic, Bronze Age, and Iron Age cultures. Some believed it was part of the ancient kingdom of Funan, the Tambalingam mentioned in old Buddhist texts, on the migration route from the area now known as Cambodia and Vietnam. Along the banks of the Tembeling River, Bronze Age drums, bells, and iron parangs had been found. When the air was especially still and silent there were people living along the riverbank who claimed to have heard the sounds of tinkling bells, the clanging of molten metal being fashioned into precious goods.

Steps led down to the jetty. Here their guides and boatmen, Kasim and Arif, were waiting next to a long, flat-bottomed wooden boat with an awning for protection from the sun.

Soon they were crossing the swirling waters, pointing the motor-powered boat into the midstream of the Tembeling River.

As they left the hustle and bustle of human activity behind, the noises of the jungle took over. The bird calls seemed louder; the hooting of gibbons echoed across the river valley. Amanda was sitting next to Cheng. He said little, staring out at the landscape. She didn't mind, as she was looking about her in all directions, trying not to miss anything. Hisham sat in front with Faridah, where he made an enthusiastic guide who kept turning round to point things out; a monitor lizard clambering up the bank to escape the wash of the boat, the Neran trees leaning over the riverbanks and, further away, the taller Dipterocarp trees that cover most of Malaysia. Hisham told her 'di' means two, 'ptero' means wings and 'carp' means seeds – seeds with two wings, allowing them to be dispersed by air and water. Here and there were signs of settlement: a couple of attap houses, people bathing or doing their laundry on the riverbank, someone fishing. The sun was getting low when, to their relief, they could see the lights of the Rest House, their stop for the night.

That night, Amanda sat in her room in the Rest House writing up her notes, reflecting on her journey. Just a week ago she'd been deep in the Carnivorous Zone of Kew Gardens, immersed in the rows and rows of *Nepenthes*, pitcher plants, checking for species variations. *Nepenthes*, from the Greek *ne* for 'no' and *penthos* 'sorrow', known to the western world as far back as Homer's *Odyssey*. She'd long had a fascination with this plant, ever since she'd brought a little pot home from Woolworths, putting it on the kitchen window to catch the flies. At some point Derek from Orchids had popped his head round the door, spotted her behind a giant Venus flytrap and called out, 'Amanda, the chief wants you.'

The route to the main office block passed beds of summer flowers flush with roses, lavender, towering agapanthus, bergamot, and marguerites, all nodding in the mid-summer sun. Sitting in front of the director, her head full of floral images, she didn't at first hear what he was saying. She was being sent to Malaysia. A possible new species had been identified by the Malaysian Botanical Society and an invitation had been extended to Kew to join the team to verify it. Amanda was the obvious choice. Amanda had never travelled beyond Europe before. The opportunity had never come up. Now, with just a week's notice, she was on the other side of the world.

That night she tossed and turned, images of the past few days racing around her head. Her dreams were full of random images – being chased by the grumpy shopkeeper, finding a monitor lizard sitting on her bed, walking through busy streets of metal workers, surrounded by the rhythmic clanging and ringing of metal against metal, the sound louder and louder till she woke with a start to the sound of the ceiling fan grinding in its case as it spun round and round.

It was an early start, the sun just rising above the trees on the horizon. Amanda made her way to the steps of the Rest House, munching sandwiches left out for breakfast. Their guide Kasim was there, talking intensely in Malay to Cheng, with Arif close by. Kasim and Arif greeted Amanda politely. Cheng looked away, seemingly irritated at being interrupted. Kasim and Arif seemed remarkably underdressed for a jungle walk in flipflops, shorts, and a singlet, while Cheng wore khaki shorts and trainers. It made her wonder whether she was overdressed in her long-sleeved T-shirt, cargo trousers, and desert boots. When Hisham and Faridah emerged also covered from head to toe, she felt less conspicuous.

Hisham walked up to Cheng and Kasim, looking displeased. Seeing Amanda looking at him he transformed his frown into a charming smile. 'You know, many of the Malays living here still keep the animistic beliefs of their forefathers,' he said. 'Kasim is worried that the place we are going to is a place with spiritual importance for the Batek people, the Orang Asli tribe that still live in the forest. But we city people don't believe in that kind of thing. *Mari*, come, let's go.' And off he strode.

Amanda had read a bit about the Batek people of the rainforest. Before leaving she'd found some dusty journals on Malaysia in the library. They believed *hantu*, spirits, lived in everything – trees, plants, animals. Birds were important as they carried the souls of the newborn and those of the departed. The soul lived on in the shadows of the night and became the flitting shadows of the forest. Sometimes the spirits were benign. Sometimes they were destroyers, causing people harm. The spirit of the underworld was a water snake. If you upset him, you might drown. Hornbills, those large birds with a casque on their beaks, were gods of the upper world. She agreed with Hisham and didn't believe in this kind of thing either but out of respect for Kasim tried to look noncommittal.

Kasim led them through the staff *kampong*, past a *sepak raga* pitch, past women hanging out washing, smiling, and calling out greetings of '*Selamat hari*'. Then they were in the jungle. Almost immediately Amanda felt its power. Tall rainforest trees blocked out the light so that it was now quite dark and the air was cooler. Noises were more acute. Leaves rustled; twigs snapped. Somewhere among the trees, you could hear the tock tock sound of a woodpecker knocking on bark, the continuous drone of insects, clicking noises, like electricity, and birds calling to each other, flitting in and out of branches.

They were following the Sungai Tahan, the river that rises in Gunung Tahan, West Malaysia's highest mountain. Glimpses of the river could be seen sparkling below through the trees. Their destination was Batu Kera, or Monkey Rock, a crop of limestone hills where the pitcher plants had first been spotted.

Hisham told her that the Malays called pitcher plants *periuk kera*, meaning monkey cups. She thought that delightfully apt. They did look like little beakers, just the right size for monkeys to drink from.

Kasim led the way. It was hard to chat in single file, so they walked mostly in silence. Amanda kept stopping, exclaiming over plants she had only ever seen in the tropical house at Kew. Cheng, softening under her enthusiasm, patiently told her some of the names. He pointed out the tall meranti trees, prized for their hard wood, now critically endangered. The tualang trees, favoured by honeybees. The jelutong, a hardwood that can grow around sixty metres high and has a white latex that, mixed with poison, is used in blowpipes.

Unexpectedly the path opened out into a clearing where they found themselves in a Batek camp of six small shelters surrounding a low, smoking fire. Each shelter had a raised platform about five feet long, with attap roofs and walls of bark for protection. A woman on a platform was nursing a young child. Others were busy around the camp whittling, stoking the fire, chopping and making things from wood.

The botanists greeted them respectfully in Malay. One of the Batek called out to Kasim, speaking a different language. A heated discussion ensued. Kasim looked troubled and spoke sorrowfully to Hisham. Turning to Amanda and Cheng, Hisham explained that the man had told them that Batu Kera was a sacred site and they should make an offering before climbing. 'What kind of offering?' Amanda wanted to know, but Hisham refused to answer, as if he were embarrassed.

The sun was high in the sky now, the temperature rising. Rivulets of sweat crawled down Amanda's face and neck. Soon she had run out of tissues to mop herself. In front, Cheng had what looked like a little hand towel round his neck with the words 'Good Morning' printed across the edge. Every so often, he used this to mop his brow. Amanda envied him.

They started to climb away from the river. The path was narrower, overgrown with tall grasses, saplings, creepers. Ahead, Kasim was using his parang to clear the way. As they walked, Amanda felt something on her shin, like the brush of a nettle or a twig poking her. She stopped and lifted the edge of her trousers. A dark, slug-like creature hung from her shin. Exposed, it lifted its head and waved it at her. Shrieking, she tried to brush it away, but it stuck fast. Alerted by her screams, the rest of the group stopped in alarm. Arif reached over and flicked the creature off with his parang. '*Pacat*,' he called out to Kasim.

Cheng explained it was a leech. 'But how did it get through my trousers,' Amanda wailed, 'and past the leech barrier I smeared on.'

'They're impossible to keep out completely,' Cheng said. 'That's why I wear shorts. I can just flick them off as I walk along. Don't worry. The bleeding will stop. It may just be a bit itchy for a few days.'

Wailing from Faridah and exclamations from Hisham announced they had discovered leeches on them, too. While she waited, Amanda took the opportunity to check for more leeches and have a swig of water. The level in her bottle was low. She had better pace herself. It wasn't clear when she could next get a refill. As she stood there, Arif pointed out the leeches around them. They were looping along the leaves of the undergrowth, waving in the air, trying to get a hold of any passing creature. She shuddered.

The ground got rockier as they climbed. At one point Amanda heard a chuffing sound, getting faster and faster before ending in a loud, evil cackle. 'Hornbill,' she was told. High above she could hear rustling and some clicking noises and just about make out the plumage of the bird, the strange casque bobbing as it pecked at the berries on the tree. It looked imposing and regal, as a god should, but thankfully felt benign and unthreatening.

Eventually they emerged from the trees on to a plateau. In front of them rose a series of jagged cliffs, the limestone hills of Batu Kera, Monkey Rock. Trails of creepers hung down from ledges and crevices. Gaping mouths hinted at possible caves. Amanda could see why pitcher plants would like it here. They do well in infertile soil, with good drainage. Deep fissures appeared in the rock, as they gradually climbed higher and higher. Reaching a stretch of flat ground, Kasim stopped and told them it was around here that the new species had been seen and where the botanists he had been guiding took the photographs that had alerted Hisham.

They were exposed now to the full force of the burning sun, so retreated to the shade of an overhang. They had a bite to eat and discussed what to do next. Hisham suggested they split up. He would go to the west with Faridah while Amanda and Cheng went to the east. Kasim and Arif would stay here with their rucksacks. Cheng looked unhappy and Amanda tried not to take it personally. Having rested, they headed in different directions. After a few yards, Cheng said to Amanda, 'Why don't you concentrate here, and I'll see what the terrain looks like further on. If I see anything I'll call you.' Amanda agreed. She could see Cheng felt embarrassed at being alone with her.

She was on a broad ledge following the edge of a cliff. On one side a sheer drop plummeted to the jungle below. On the other, a rock face rose hundreds of feet. Between here and the next range of limestone hills lay a valley of rainforest trees. After that, the Tahan mountain range stretched out to the horizon.

A stillness surrounded her, almost as if the heat had sent all living creatures into the shade, where they would stay until the sun dropped and the air cooled. Further on, the ledge opened up to an uneven plateau. Without the shade of the overhang the rays of the sun were burning, but she was determined to play her part. She placed her hat firmly on her head, took a swig of water and strode out. Plants trailed down from cracks in the rock. *Nepenthes macfarlanei,* occurring only in Malaysia. And was that a *Nepenthes sanguinea*? She examined the tendrils, the pointed leaves, softly brushed the speckled funnels, the monkey cups, enjoyed their velvety feel, peered in for insects. She was so absorbed she hadn't noticed that she was actually quite a long way from where she started. She was only dragged out of her reverie by finding herself on the edge of a deep gully about twenty feet deep and too wide to jump across. She looked down. Wait, wasn't that a *Nepenthes ramispina*? The plant winked and nodded at her. She had to go down.

The walls of the gully were steep. It would be a scramble, but possible. Sitting on the ground she lowered herself over the edge, finding footholds before sliding down the last few feet in a cascade of stone and dust. Pitcher plants were growing out of small crevasses in the rocks, just within reach. It was strange seeing the plants in their natural habitat surrounded by moss and ferns. They looked so healthy and happy, she thought to herself. This one was a lovely specimen. The exterior of the funnels was the colour of old burgundy, the colour of midnight, of mystery, of secrets. In contrast the colour inside was a fresh lime green. A clean colour, open and transparent. The leaves were a glossy dark green. She examined each of the pitchers, lovingly running her hands over them. As she did so, there was something about the peristome that made her take a closer look. There was an extra curl that she hadn't seen before. Could this be the plant they were looking for? She took a few photos and then looked around her. The sun was lower, the bottom of the gully darkening fast. She realised she should go back and join the others. But the walls of the gully were steep and she couldn't find a foothold. She tried climbing with her feet straddling both sides of the rock face but kept slipping down. She had to get out somehow. She couldn't risk getting stuck here, needing to be rescued. It would be so humiliating. She shuffled along the gully looking for a way up.

She was parched, her water bottle empty, the darkening gully making her nervous. She started to think of the creatures that might live in the gully. Nocturnal snakes and lizards. The night shadows – the souls of the dead. She gave a whimper and started shouting, 'Help, help.'

Above her, in the cool of the late afternoon, the jungle was coming alive again. The screeching and calling of birds, the electric drone of cicadas, the whining of insects, knocking sounds, monkeys hooting and whooping. She was on the verge of despair when she noticed a figure standing above her. Tall and slender, he stood on the edge of the gully quietly looking down, observing her. An Orang Asli, naked save for a loin cloth round his waist, a blowpipe in his right hand. Her stomach lurched and she repressed the scream rising in her. 'Stay calm,' she told herself, 'stay calm,' and waved tentatively, hoping this was a universally understood gesture. Then remembering what she'd seen Hisham do earlier on in the camp, she put her hand on her chest and bowed. Almost imperceptibly, he inclined his head. He stood there for a bit longer then put his blowpipe aside, lay on the ground and reached down.

Amanda hesitated. Was he offering to pull her up? Was he strong enough and was she up to it? She had no choice but to try. By wedging herself against the sides of the ravine, she was able to reach up and grab his outstretched hand. It was strong and firm, crushing her fingers. Using his arm as a rope she scrambled up a couple of feet. Without warning, he yanked her up the final distance, leaving her sprawling on the side of the gorge. She got up trembling, gabbling at him in the only bit of Malay she knew. '*Terima kasih*, thank you, thank you,' she kept repeating. He said something and pointed, making it clear that was the direction she needed to go, then silently disappeared into the undergrowth. Shaking, she made her way back in the direction she had come. Rounding a corner, she saw Hisham and Kasim. Overjoyed to be safe and to have found the group, she ran towards them. But things did not look good. Faridah was sitting on the floor weeping hysterically, while Cheng sat in a daze, covered in blood.

Hisham looked up as she approached, relief flooding his face. 'Thank goodness, at least you are safe and well,' he said and looked as if he could hug her. He explained what had happened. Cheng had seen a clump of pitcher plants growing by a rock face. Trying to get a closer look, he had walked into a clump of rattan. Rattan has long spines covered with razor sharp thorns. The more he tried to disentangle himself, the more he became entangled. The thorns ripped his flesh, his arms, his bare legs, his face. Kasim and Arif found him screaming in pain. They cut him loose with their parangs, trying not to get scratched themselves. He was losing blood at a dangerous speed. His wounds were too severe to leave to heal in the tropical climate – they could get septic and gangrenous. Arif had been sent back to summon help using the nearest phone at the Rest House. Meanwhile, Faridah had been bitten by a snake. They didn't think it was poisonous, but they couldn't risk not having it checked. Someone had bound a tourniquet round her foot but she couldn't step on it.

They had already arranged to stay the night in the home of a local Malay couple. The group would go as planned and wait there for help. Darkness descends rapidly when the sun goes down in the tropics. They needed to get going. Kasim and Hisham formed a human crutch supporting Cheng. Faridah leant on Amanda and hopped along with the help of a stick. Progress was slow. It was now dark. Roots and low-lying branches blocked their way. After an hour they saw light glinting through the trees and emerged into a small clearing. Figures rushed towards them, a man and woman. Without understanding what they were saying, Amanda recognised their concern and kindness. The woman took Faridah's free arm and helped Amanda carry her the final steps. 'Hatun,' she said, introducing herself.

The house was a traditional, rural Malay house, raised on stilts as a protection from flooding and animals. The entrance was up a crude ladder, resting at a low angle, rungs spaced widely apart. Family members ran up and down without difficulty, but Amanda struggled to stay erect and crawled up on her hands and knees. Cheng and Faridah were hauled up, groaning and yelling in pain.

They left their shoes at the doorway and entered a large room. Woven mats covered bare boards. Everything happened in this one room. Faridah and Cheng were laid in a corner to rest. In the centre, a meal of rice, fried fish, and greens was laid out on the floor for the others. The rice and greens were grown by the couple, Hisham told her, and the fish caught in the river nearby. Normally Amanda would have tucked in with relish, appreciating the freshness of the food, its local provenance. But at this moment she was confused and very, very tired. All she wanted to do was lie down, sleep, and forget the excitement of the day. Fully clothed she lay down next to Faridah, wrapped herself in her sarong and tried to block out the outside world.

She slept badly. The night sounds of the jungle were deafening. Persistent screeching, banging on the roof, scratching and slithering below. Was that the roar of a tiger, an elephant? And the sounds of Cheng's groans and Faridah's moans.

A whirring noise outside roused her. A helicopter had come to take Cheng and Faridah to the nearest hospital, an eight-hour trip by boat, but a mere hour or so by air. The helicopter flew off, leaving Hisham, Amanda, Kasim and Arif behind. They had a task to complete – verifying this new species of *Nepenthes*. Amanda's photos and Cheng's samples would not be enough. It had to be verified in situ. Hatun handed over a bundle. Food for the journey. Amanda thanked her, feeling tongue-tied and inadequate, unable to express her gratitude to the good people who had opened up their home and shared the little they had.

In the daylight it was only a short walk to where they had been the day before. Out of the corner of her eye, Amanda caught a glimpse of Kasim and Arif leaving some rice and fish under the overhang – an offering to the Monkey God. The rattan had been cleared, and they soon found the plants Cheng had spotted. After a careful inspection, both Hisham and Amanda agreed it was a new species. Samples were taken and carefully placed in a special airtight container. Then they walked back to the Rest House.

The next day, Amanda was reclining in the launch on her way back to the train station. Many of the plants and trees they passed were now pleasantly familiar. She could actually identify some of them. While she feasted her eyes on the greenery, she reflected on the previous day's events and the warnings the Batek, Kasim and Arif had given them about Monkey Rock. The Monkey God lives there, they had warned, don't upset him. How they had dismissed these fears as superstitious nonsense. The trip had nearly been a disaster. She had got lost and two people had been severely injured. She had thought these animistic views nothing but the beliefs of primitive people, quaint relics of the past, having nothing to do with the scientific, rational world she was part of, a world that took pride in its logic, objectivity, and evidence.

She sat up straight. But of course, the Batek people were right! Gods and spirits of the natural world appear in all cultures in the form of nymphs, dryads, sirens, djinns, and kelpies. They exist to remind humans to treat nature with respect. Amanda and her fellow botanists had been arrogant. They hadn't listened to the people who knew the area. Their experiences yesterday showed that if you didn't do this, you would suffer the consequences. The 'gods' would chastise you in some way. Their group hadn't paid attention to the dangers of the area, listened to the warnings, or learnt what to look out for, the creatures that lived there, the plants that could hurt you. And they had paid the price.

DOG ROSES

TAMAR HODES

A single white camellia led to our worst ever row.

We were leaving Charlie and Adam's house after one of those wonderful evenings where time dissolves like the sun slipping easily into the sea. Maybe it was Charlie's French onion broth crowned with dripping, cheesy bread, or the conversation about travel and film, but our laughter and storytelling defied the clock. It was after 2 a.m. when we eventually left, none of us wanting to end the discussion. Before our hosts waved us on our way, they put on the outside light, easing us from the warmth of their candlelit company to the cold of the early morning. Charlie and Adam gently shut the door, probably to go and stack the dishwasher, set it into action and slip, tired but happy, together into their bed.

We strolled through their narrow garden, the light throwing a mysterious glow over the dark foliage. A camellia bush with waxy leaves, glossily brazen in the half-darkness, offered its white flowers as night lights marking the path. As we passed the bush, Ginny brushed the leaves with her hand and then suddenly grabbed a bloom, snapped the twig supporting it and walked on.

'Why did you do that?' I hissed.

'Ssh,' she laughed.

I lowered my voice but repeated my question. 'What did you do that for?'

'Don't be such an old maid,' she said. 'It's only one flower. It doesn't matter.'

'But it's theirs,' I protested. 'You shouldn't have taken it.'

Suddenly our delightful evening curdled and we didn't speak in the car on the way home, in the house or even in our bed, where we lay on a taut sheet with our backs to each other and a cold space between us.

This was not the first time that Ginny had shocked me. When I first met her, it was like dating a feral animal. She would run barefoot on the beach dangling her sandals in her hands, ribboning in and out of the sea. She'd thread daisies and scatter them in her hair. She'd rip the crust off bread rather than slicing it with a knife, dropping large, spongy pieces in her mouth, laughing as she ate them. In bed or on the floor or in the bathroom or wherever our lovemaking occurred, she was the most uninhibited partner I had had. She offered her body to me like a book open at its centre, letting me in. There were no boundaries with Ginny: everything was possible. It was what I loved – and loathed – about her.

But we often rowed and the arguments were always about this one issue: she would take what I didn't feel she had a right to. In restaurants, she would grasp a spoon, slipping its glinting silver secretly into her bag, or she'd remove a plate, a wine glass, or anything else she found attractive. In an art gallery, once, Ginny took a catalogue without paying for it, when the attendant was momentarily distracted.

Once home, she put the shiny camellia in a glass on the kitchen window sill as if to parade her illicit wares. Each time I passed it, its glossy whiteness seemed to wink at me, reminding me of her theft. I began to wonder: where would her thieving end? Would she take a lover from a friend? Would she steal someone else's husband? Would she lift a baby from a pram?

There was the seaside incident. We had had a great time collecting white shells from the beach, eating fish and chips perched upon a wall while gazing out at the crashing waves, covering each other with love in the B&B, ignoring the ghastly floral wallpaper and laughing at the plastic flowers cemented in a fake shell.

We were about to leave and then it happened again. Ginny slipped the miniature shampoo and bubble bath bottles in her bag: fine. But then she took one of the towels, 'Bay View' embroidered on it in red, and slipped it into her holdall.

'What are you doing, Ginny?' I asked, as if I didn't know. I had that gnawing in the pit of my stomach that her thieving always gave me.

'Everyone does it,' she answered.

'No,' I argued, feeling the happy days sour. 'A bottle of shampoo, maybe, but not a towel. You always take it too far.'

'You're ridiculous, Matt,' she laughed. 'Your strict moral code. You're so Victorian.'

'That's your defence. To ridicule me.'

'Ridicule? You sound like a character from Dickens. Who even speaks like that?'

I began to feel anxious each time we went out. A shoe shop, a gallery, a chemist, a grocers: all of these made me scared that she was going to take something that wasn't hers. I felt I couldn't trust her. When she brought shopping home, I'd search the bag for the receipt and check it against her goods. Part of me wanted to shop her to the police; another part of me wanted her to get away with it as I loved her.

In spite of a shaky few months together, we decided it was time to meet the parents. Ginny's family home was ramshackle chaos. The front garden (if you could call it that) of the Victorian terrace was a jungle: long grasses, unkempt weeds tangling and knotting each other like unbrushed hair, the window sills unpainted and cracked, half the tiles missing so that the roof looked like a dentally neglected mouth, the outside of the house a reliable indicator of the tip inside. There were some lovely charcoal drawings, ceramic pots, and hundreds of books reclining on any surface they could find. Drawers were left open; piles of washing lay everywhere. Curtains hung awkwardly from broken rods. Fruit shone blue with mould in dusty bowls. Her parents were friendly enough, her stepdad's beard as tangled as the garden; her mum, wearing a colourful dress and brightly coloured wooden beads, was warm and effusive but I noticed that her nails were dirty. Food-encrusted pots bubbled on the stove. Lunch, which arrived after four o'clock, was a combination of mismatched options: hummus, salads, vegetables that I didn't recognise, rice congealed in sticky balls, dishes served cold when they really needed heating, meat in glossy sauces that I worried would give me food poisoning. There was laughter and discussion and if you wanted to speak, you had to create a space for yourself. Photos slipping out of ill-fitting frames revealed half-siblings and multiple marriages so complicated that even Ginny seemed unsure of her own genealogy. I sensed that her parents found me stiff: the more liberal their comments, the more buttoned-up I felt, their looseness bringing out the fogey in me.

My parents' home could not have been more different. Ginny stared in horror at the ubiquitous cream and beige theme. Every object from a teaspoon to a photograph to a tea towel had a place, be it in a drawer or frame or cupboard. My parents were civil to Ginny but I could sense my mother's disapproval at her floral bandana stretched across her forehead, her long top that couldn't decide if it was a tunic or a dress, and her loud laugh. My parents looked as if a wild pony had galloped through their pristine home. Lunch was bland and Ginny unsubtly ground salt and pepper onto her food as if desperately willing it to have some flavour. There was no conversation, just an occasional commentary on the food such as 'The meat's nice and tender' or 'The potatoes turned out well'. My parents referred frequently to my older sister, who had married an accountant, produced two dull children, and owned a tidy house and a big car; even the petunias in her front garden were colour-coded.

Ginny's mum, Dru, volunteered at the donkey sanctuary, so one day we went there. To my mind, the donkeys were a mangy lot: large, doleful eyes, straggly coats, skinny bodies, and the place stank like a sewer. Ginny chatted happily to the volunteers and stroked the donkeys. It seemed to me that she was as comfortable among the urine-soaked straw as she was in an art gallery. As Dru, in her wellies, mucked out the stables, fed the animals and brushed their manky sides, she looked as unkempt as the donkeys. She was clearly a good woman, devoting her time to others: running drama workshops in prisons, helping out in schools in deprived areas. I couldn't help feeling, maybe uncharitably, that she should have spent more time with her daughter and stepchildren, enforcing some boundaries.

'Matt,' laughed Ginny. 'The donkeys love you.'

'Really?' I said, miserably.

When Ginny and I arrived home that evening and showered, trying to scrub the poo and straw smell from our fingertips, we fell into bed and I was grateful that Ginny knew no barriers. We only stopped our kissing long enough for me to tell her that she stank like a donkey and we laughed.

On another occasion we met my parents at the fruit farm, my folks in matching blue anoraks and Ginny in one of her don't-know-if-it's-a-dress-or-top outfits, bandana orbiting her head and a cornflower tucked behind one ear.

'Alan! Sue!' she called as she ran to embrace them. They did their ironing board imitations and did not bend to her hug. Mum and Dad had a system for fruit picking: up one side, down the other. Ginny skipped from row to row, spending more time eating and licking than actually putting anything in her punnet. Her fingers looked as if she had dipped them into a bottle of red ink and her lips were pink and swollen.

As my parents' punnets filled up, I could see them looking at each other and I knew what those exchanges meant. They thought that Ginny was out of control, and I knew that her parents probably found me stiff. Was this ever going to work?

Standing at the edge of the field, watching my parents' regimental routine and Ginny's haphazard skipping, I froze. I didn't know which side to join. I found myself doing nothing and I felt desperate: a school teacher who wanted to write a novel but had never quite managed it, a man in his mid-thirties who had not committed to anyone, someone who was still trying to work out who he was. Watching Ginny's body weaving in and out of the leafy rows, I wondered what on earth someone so delightful and vivacious could possibly see in me. When I was with her, she seemed to release the person I was hoping I might be one day.

Wracked by indecision, I chose neither option but stayed, punnet empty, rooted to the spot until they all returned to me, like kids completing a treasure hunt to show their spoils. My parents' punnets were full, the beady raspberries blinking in the sun. Ginny's fruit seemed squashed, as if the ruby spheres had congealed into a sticky mess.

Back at my parents' home, we washed the fruit in their white kitchen, boiled the globes before straining them until the pips stuck miserably in the sieve, and put them into jars. My mother had cut out little green-and-white-checked cloth tops and unnecessary 'Raspberry Jam' labels. I was worried that Ginny would put her sticky fingers on Mum's work surface or that she would say something inappropriate or steal one of Mum's figurines. I was pleased when we got home, Ginny clutching her labelled jar from my mum as if she had won the tombola. Ginny unscrewed the lid and dipped her finger in.

'It's not ready yet,' I said. 'It has to set.'

'Oh,' said Ginny, dabbing a blob of jam on my nose, 'how I love you and all your little regulations. Kiss me.'

The camellia incident left a bad taste in my mouth for weeks. Each time we had to recover from an argument it became harder. Ginny progressed with her dissertation; I taught my classes. I found it hard to concentrate. I felt torn in two. I could marry someone sensible and live a beige and cream life like my parents. Or I could stay with Ginny and we would love and dance and sing but she would shock me from time to time by her flouting of rules, by her feral galloping into forbidden places.

One day, Ginny came back from the garden centre with dog roses. From a brown paper bag, she drew out a rambling plant, the flat pink flowers wobbling on stalks like little plates. I watched from the kitchen window as she dug a hole in the earth. Her hands were caked with mud. In the hole, she placed the bush. The roses danced around her head as if she were wearing the flowers in her hair, as if she had lost herself happily in the plant.

The relationship, I felt, was grinding to a halt. Although I loved her, I saw obstacles lining our future like black lanterns at the edge of the path: the wedding, the children, the many decisions that lay ahead of us were going to be laden with difficulty and conflict. Every step would be hazardous, my family not agreeing with Ginny and hers not agreeing with me. I felt bleak.

Washing the plates, I gloomily recalled my failed relationships: Corrie, an actress, dedicated to her work but not to me; Rowena, fun but unreliable; Sheila, who my parents loved but I didn't; and Naomi, who took but gave nothing back. I felt love flooding back to Ginny. I watched her straighten up and admire the bush, her face brightening. Her green wellies were too big for her so that she looked like a little girl, in borrowed (or stolen) boots. Her hair was scrunched into a messy bun, her cheeks were pink, her flowery dress hung unevenly below her coat. I thought, she belongs to no season and to every season. She looks as if she has grown out of the soil.

I abandoned my washing up, leaving the dishes shipwrecked in foamy water, and felt my body fall towards her as if she were a magnet calling me, drawing me through the glass, over the lawn and to her side. I lifted Ginny up, my arms around her waist, and I spun her round and round till we were both giddy with the spinning. She laughed and threw her head back as if she were on a carousel, her hair flying in the air. Although we were dancing, my mouth found hers and we kissed, determined that our lips would stay together.

Above and around us, the dog roses sprang and bounced, refusing to be tamed, free, their dusty pink discs leaping this way.

And that.

MULCH

REBECCA FERRIER

Ah, the carpet needed watering again! The squelch was off. It had to be *loud*, it had to be *ripe*, it had to be *ready*. Jay tugged the garden hose around her bedroom. Here, silverfish slept in corners and spiders held the rafters high with elaborate weaves. Onwards, the hose went, scraping the hall's floorboards. Smell that? Rot and ruin, sporing into lungs. A damp smell, a good smell.

There's life in that, there is.

Plants don't speak. That's why Jay liked them, loved them, tended to them until they grew as tall as her head and as thick as her thigh. Rumour was she'd grown a baby once. It had howled and mizzled and gummed its displeasure across her meadowed sanctuary.

No use, no good – fertiliser.

Her plants were all that Jay could never be. Succulent, rare, green. Unattainable descriptors, like: 'Comes back better year after year! A show of colour! Great for bedding!' This was not – never had been, never will be – Jay. The skin at her joints was sagged, while her complexion sank to a tuber's hue. Her chin was whiskered white and melded into a bullfrog's neck, hiding the collar to her faded, floral blouse. It was a lucky shirt, worn last September at the Pilton Village Grower's Fair.

First Prize: Marrow.

'There's none to beat it,' the head judge had said, mouth a-twist with envy. Her reward: applause muted through gardening gloves, a bright ribbon, and suspicion as narrow as a stem. Next came the be-suited men and soil samples, the visitors in visors and the questions, questions, questions. Because her green thumb was too green and a cut to her quick did not run red.

Jay's cottage was cultivated in a quiet valley's inner elbow, wet and dark and forested. When the March rains came to Devon, the fields swelled and washed her road to a river. With a pendulum's walk, Jay would find the deepest part, where two skies pressed upon the same horizon. Once the ripples stilled, she found nature's true mirror. There, her muddy reflection. A hag with only fog and frogs for company. Her plants were no extension, though she willed them to be. She belonged to no one, not even the upside-down Jay staring right at her through the puddle-pond depths.

If she thought kindly on herself – a rarity – she could say her tangled hair had an ivy's strength and her face was as down-turned as a hellebore's. But these were not petalled traits, no social currency for a twenty-first century, no love.

This here's mulch, only mulch.

When the track to her cottage was dry, the postman delivered bills, junk mail and letters from Jay's city-dwelling daughter: 'Sell the dump and live with me! It's not healthy. We'll get a good price. For god's sake, Mum! It's not like you need the money.' Opened, then placed upon the compost heap.

Knotweed, that's all she is, thought Jay. *An invasive species.*

No, it hadn't been worth it, that teenage quickie behind the waltzers with a ticket-seller. He had been flinchingly kind, in a bullied, acne-prone way. Squelching grass, a dew-wet bottom, nervous hands in her school uniform and broken knicker elastic. Her first and last. Jay's parents had shown displeasure and, in return, Jay had grown her own, its Latin name *Atropa belladonna*. This poisonous perennial could be found in between the shed and the tomato bed. It put the aged couple (and their ever-aspiring middle-class disappointment) to rest. After the funeral, the cob-walled cottage – now sodden and steaming – was left to Jay and her unborn child.

When pregnant and harbouring the fleshy seedling, Jay had pictured them – she and her daughter – running together. Wild-lings, calling as curlews, loping across moorland. Knuckles bruised with beach rock, heather braided into their tangled manes, suppers baked atop salt-split driftwood ('See the flames in sea colours, m'girl!'). Singing songs only the beasts knew, the pair would dine on tender gulls, pickled limpets, and the season's first gorse flowers.

It was not meant to be, for the sprog had disliked the outdoors. Whined it was all cold and wet and muck. She saw isolation where Jay knew freedom. And this child, her own and ever-distant, sneezed in the pollen-heavy months, puckered red at tree sap, and grew a heart as hard as conker. Worse still, she gazed at herself, rather than the garden. Because she, this daughter, was a pretty creature. Jay could nurture those; tend them to loveliness and never discover that for herself.

No matter now, Jay had sowed a solution.

She had planted Him.

In the conservatory was a long box. Six-four in length (soon to be height) and heaped with nitrogen-rich, banana-peeled soil. Jay flattened her palms to the trough, the hose now discarded.

'You've grown, m'love,' she cooed. 'Oh, how we'll run and rut as wild-lings –'

BRING, the doorbell shouted.

'Nearly time,' she promised. 'Nearly ready.'

On the porch were unwell-meaning sounds. Hard shoes, distant voices. Youths? No, it couldn't be. Those wastrels threw stones, broke windows, called names: 'Freak, witch, ugly.' Children were easy to scare off, and she *liked* to scare them (and catch and poke). But what waited on the door's other side was a woman. Bleach-blonde clean, microfibre skirt tucked tightly around her rear, and a government-issue clipboard. Jay clawed a fleece around her shoulders and breathed into her net curtains.

'Mrs Irving? I'm Francis from Social Services.'

Her elongated vowels came through the letterbox in a corkscrew.

Jay's toes curled thickly inside her Wellington boots. Garden shears, their varnish worn to a memory, settled in her hands. She had sliced stalks and roots and branches with these: a sapless young woman would be no trouble, none at all.

'There's no answer,' said Francis to another. 'Take down the door, Donald.'

'We'll get in trouble,' was the reply, wet as a watering can. 'Isn't that breaking and entering? Legally, we can't survey the land until −'

'She might've had a fall.'

'I suppose it *is* our duty to save her.'

'No, it ain't!' Jay wound the chain across the door and eased it open, pressing her face through the three-inch gap. 'You're from Bio-What or Syni-Who,' she howled. 'Corporate rights! − genetic modifications! − soil suckers! − plant pinchers!'

Ever since the Pilton Village Grower's Fair there had been unwanted attention. Queries and post, telephone requests − wrenched out, line dead − and calls and calls and calls.

'What plants are those, Mrs Irving?' Francis wore a mouth that spoke without speaking. It said she'd fornicated in fur coats and sucked Martini-soaked olives with high-shine lips. She was ill-placed on the garden path. Midges spun circles above her head. Her heels − red-soled − sank into the gravel, milli-pede-metre by milli-pede-metre, as though the soil (and all its critters) intended to close its maw around her.

It'd spit her out again, there's no mulch in her, nothing that'd rot good.

Jay squeezed her shears tighter and pressed her thighs together.

Oh, to grow a body like that.

'I met those polyester slugs the other day,' said Jay, recalling their wires and beeps and fearful technology. 'Came trampling my begonias and shovin' cuttings into *plastic* bags.'

'We need to see your living conditions,' the man, Donald, spoke this time. 'Be a dear and let us in?'

'We can help, Mrs Irving,' said Francis.

Was this what Jay's own daughter looked like? Smeared with a sunless tan, bright contacts pressed into corneas, lashes wilting with too-thick mascara. Here was a hybrid rose, clad in ice-cream colours, who would not survive the winter.

'I've called the police, I have,' she said, 'and they'll be here soon, they will.'

'There's no need, Mrs Irving.'

'It'll take Officer Reid fifteen minutes to get 'ere from the village, I timed him once,' said Jay. She shelled the mistruth from her mouth as one might shuck a pea. 'Arrested your last bunch, didn't he? I saw right through them, too, with their *laminated* badges.' Oh, how she had crowed when their Land Rover sped off, fearing sirens and slow, rural bureaucracy. 'You going to offer me ten grand or twenty, this time?'

No one could afford Him. Anxiety clotted Jay's nostrils. He was unripe and unfinished. *No one can take Him.* He was all she had – *would have* – to belong to.

'I'm from Social Services,' repeated Francis, whose stretched nails, *STOP*-sign red, extended forwards. 'I'll pop the kettle on and we'll have a natter.'

Jay's own hands were broken. Her nail's undersides frowned with mud. Thorn marks, liver spots, shovel shapes: a mole's tools. The question was, would He notice? There was a rawness to her knuckles she'd failed to scrub out. Or was scrubbing the problem? She hadn't scrubbed before Him, took no care as to what she looked like before Him.

Nearly time, I must be ready, nearly here –

'Mrs Irving?'

Here came the *CRUNCH* as Jay slammed the door. Then *SNAP* as Jay's shears went a-trimming. Shellacked digits *PLOD, PLOD, PLOD*-ed on the wet, wet welcome mat. It was as quick as dead-heading marigolds. *SCREAMING.* Close, then vanishing. Now there'd be no further visitors. Nothing to disturb her – and Him – together.

'That'll teach you.'

For coming here, being beautiful, showing off.

Now no one had nice hands. This was fair. And if He didn't know what hands were meant to look like, He wouldn't mind Jay's own grubby paws. Instead, He'd love her.

Relentlessly, passionately, unendingly.

Because she'd grown Him that way.

Jay zipped her fleece and sloshed up the dirt track to Pilton. The village had a disused school, a converted church, and a blue plaque where the library used to be. There was one teashop, unentered, where a lemon drizzle slice came with gossip as sour as the folks who ate it. From within, the tea drinkers watched Jay's progress, expressions matching the open-mouthed pansies in the planters outside. Their gasps folded mist along the wall-to-ceiling windows, until the waitress – surreptitiously – used a tea towel to wipe them down. After all, Jay rarely came to Pilton. Her steps were tracked, and needlessly, it seemed, for the mud peeling from her shoes revealed her path.

Oh, the Women's Institute would be droning on about this for weeks.

Note: Jay was no longer admitted into their talcumed bosom after she laced their Victoria sponge cake ('You ain't got no proof!') with laxative-

inducing monkshood ('Grew it me'self') upon losing out on the Best Bouquet competition. ('Bastards.')

Giftan was Jay's destination. The charity shop collected limply sewn buttons, care home clear-outs, and a gentle cupboard smell. One never knew what could be found nesting in a coat pocket, warming a sleeve, or gnawing an old turban.

'Can I help you, ma'am?' Behind a *Jackie Collins* novel was a shop girl, all nose studs and lilac purple hair. Too perky, too nice, too many questions. Here was a trap, flower-pressed between kind words.

Jay turned her back and scanned the racks. *Should've brought the shears.* Her hands sweated marks on the silks. She couldn't wear white. Too old, too laughable. What about a dress with roses and ribbons and ruddiness to match her cheeks? No, it wouldn't do. The lilac tunic with petunias? Better a sack.

Gentle as a blossom bud, the shop girl spoke again. 'Is this for a special occasion?'

Embarrassment, not known since Jay's childhood, began to warm her face. At her own appearance, her talk, her size. She never spoke to people. Didn't know how to. Never had.

Jay missed her garden.

'If it's for a wedding, choose the blue.' A thoughtful pause, then, 'Yeah, I reckon you'd do well nice in blue.'

Jay's hair was brushed to bushiness and her face washed bright. The blue Giftan dress was buttoned up and looked – dare she think it – nice (the March rains had told her so). She was ready, as was He. Afternoon sun branched haphazardly into the conservatory. Above, the clear roof was mottled red and brown and amber: church light through leaf mould.

The trough waited. It should've grown runner beans and courgettes, thick gourds, or a bamboo border. Yes, it should've, it should've.

Inside, the soil was breathing.

Up and down, up and down.

Jay could grow anything, that's what the locals said. 'Peat,' spat the head judge, once, spreading lies as manure to the mass-market farmers. Anything to make a buck, discredit her, bring her down a peg. Fool, he was, to think it was the house that did it – the soil, the feed, the mulch.

No, it was *her.*

Jay reached out. Her fingers raked the nurtured earth and stirred the worms to singing.

'There you are,' she wept. 'Oh, I've been waitin' for you.'

Every second, minute, hour; longin' for anyone who'd understand that I –

A moist hand, chilled and mushroom white, met her own. It locked around her wrist. *Oh.* This was love, wasn't it? *At long last.* A hard tug pitched her forwards, face-deep into damp earth. Here came doubt a-digging. *Is it meant to be like this?* She couldn't remember. Grit scratched her gums and dirt ballooned her cheeks. Compost muffled her coughs, as her head went under, under. There was firmness beneath. He pulled harder, two hands now, this man she'd grown. *Wait.* A heave – a tug – like wrenching a garden hose. Fuzzed roots probed her nostrils and stroked the lines beneath her breasts, tucked themselves under creases and sought her private place where shame and heat gathered. *Oh!* Her heels ran higher and wheeling kicks met only air. *Please.* Each limb was bound, vined, and rooted, for these belonged to Him now.

And it no longer mattered that she could not breathe, could not struggle, could not fight, for Jay was content.

No one had held her like this in years.

BREATHING
BECOMING MIDORI

AULIC ANAMIKA

হাজার হাজার দমের খেলা —

কোন কাহিনী আজ শোনাবো তোমায়?

একদা এক তেঁতুল গাছ

দাঁড়িয়ে ছিল একা

অনেক না, শুধু একটা।

নাম না জানা পাখি

খুব জ্বালাবে

এমন এক বাঁদর

ধরা যায়না ছোঁয়া যায়না

এমনি এক হাওয়া।

"হায়রে মানুষ, রঙ্গীন মানুষ [তুমি]

দম ফুরাইলে ঠুশ!"

I have lived a thousand stories of breath.
Which one to tell?
Once upon a time
There was a tamarind tree.
Not many but one.
Last tree standing.
My companions of breath:
A tamarind tree,
An unnamed bird,
A monkey troubling me all day long.
Slipping through my fingers
A whiff of air.
'O humans, full of colour!
One breath less,
You are gone!'

Until recently, I considered myself more of a tree person, not necessarily a plant person, and definitely not a houseplant person. As a child, I knew all about creating fictive kinships with verdant trees that stood out in the open, resisting time, weather, and human hubris. There was a grand tamarind tree in the schoolyard. I thought he was my grandfather, whom I had never met. He lived and died in a small village in East Pakistan (now Bangladesh) when my father was only 18. My grandfather was never photographed, and I never heard anything about his appearance. It was easy for me to assume that he could be a tamarind tree (Latin, *Tamarindus indica*). Why not?

My grandfather was always sun-soaked, robust, and deciduous. Standing in the middle of the capital city of Bangladesh, he could not grow in the shade. He could tolerate drought but preferred to spread his roots in moist soil. He could fix nitrogen but was known to be tender to frost, which, fortunately, he never had to experience. In Bangladesh, the temperature never fell under 10°C, not even on the coldest winter days. He offered bark, roots, flowers, fruits, and leaves filled with medicinal properties. My grandfather and I did not have much in common, though, because I never tried to grow bark, roots, flowers, fruits, or leaves. Breathing as a human was just fine.

When I left school, my grandfather did not accompany me. After leaving school, I joined and left the university. I left my parents, my hometown, and the country where I was born. I arrived at a cold city in the north where the sun never quite knew how to shine.

Three decades later, I met my grandfather again. This time he decided to be a sycamore tree (*Platane* in German, *Platanus occidentalis* in Latin). He was still robust and deciduous, but he assumed an additional property. He could withstand the winter of the Northern Hemisphere. My grandfather grew taller in Europe, to the height of a hundred feet, and stood on two trunks. He developed bumps all over his trunks, a sign of his advanced age. One of these bumps became a gigantic nose. On my way to the workplace, I stroked my grandfather's nose and shared with him all my migrant troubles. Whether a *Tetul Gachh* or tamarind tree in Dhaka or a *Platane* or sycamore tree in Berlin, my grandfather was a patient person. He listened carefully without offering me any intrusive, verbal advice.

Winter came. The snowfall never stopped. Unlike my grandfather, I was mortally afraid of the cold and begged for heating long before the heating period in the city officially started. My grandfather survived through the winter but never recovered from the next summer when the sycamore trees of Western Europe began to lose their leaves. That year, he fell ill to the anthracnose epidemic, a common fungal disease of shade trees that results in massive loss of leaves. My grandfather turned grey and died slowly, drying up from the inside.

During one of the frosty winter days later that year, a friend brought me Midori, an evergreen houseplant, thinking it might help me mourn my dead grandfather. My friend said, 'This plant is a *Frostbeule* (easy to freeze) like you! Hope you two get along!'

I said, 'I am not a plant person! I do not know how to take care of a houseplant. She will die in a month!'

My friend laughed and said, 'We'll see!'

Midori survived the winter, my carelessness, and the unfriendly visitors to my apartment. One of these visitors was a white German botanist with whom I had a complicated relationship. The botanist had the nasty habit of showing off her plant naming skills. When she stepped into my bedroom, I introduced Midori. The botanist rolled her eyes and said, 'Midori? It is a *Schefflera actinophylla*. If you have trouble pronouncing the Latin name, you can call it an umbrella tree!'

Midori must have been offended. There was suddenly a bitter and pungent smell in the air, and I felt nauseous. My botanist friend opened the windows and said, 'Your houseplant seems to be angry! Teach her some manners, especially how to behave with guests!' Midori and I looked at each other. I rolled my eyes, and Midori shot out a dried leaf with vehemence.

I had never been a plant person, but I promised that I would not let Midori die. After the visit by the arrogant botanist, I decided to educate myself more in the science of *Schefflera actinophylla*. And I was curious about the local history of naming. It turned out that the Germans had named her people way back in 1894. For the sake of Midori, I also thought I should get to know her people more intimately. Whenever I visited someone's house, I started scrutinising their evergreen houseplants and asked about their health status. These humans found me overenthusiastic and plain nosy about their houseplants. Midori continued to grow, radiating leaves, and I observed her with wonder. That is how we humans had named her people, actinophylla (with radiating leaves). Some of the descriptions of her people I found to be offensive, if not outright discriminatory. They say that *Schefflera actinophylla* is an 'aggressive plant' since the members of this genus tend to dominate the soil. Humans surely know how to project their vices to non-humans! I promised not to do that to Midori.

Midori found her place in an earthen pot at the south-east corner of my bedroom near the window overlooking the city. After five years of living together, Midori began to drop her leaves last winter. First, there were occasional dry leaves on the floor. Nothing unusual. I watered her and increased the dosage of plant nutrition fluid. Soon she began to drop fresh green leaves. I started to worry. Outside the window, winter was raging. I barely went outside the house and observed Midori with increasing anxiety and helplessness. In my desperation, I called my botanist friend, who laughed off my worries: 'It is winter! Even evergreen plants lose a few leaves. No big deal!'

Midori kept dropping her green leaves. Soon there were hardly any leaves left. I stopped going outside except to the grocery shop and the neighbourhood plant shop. The shop owner frowned at me as the frequency of my visits increased. On my tenth visit, when I did not buy anything and asked too many questions, he refused to talk to me and showed me the door. I sent a long letter to my workplace explaining that a family member was ill and that I had to take care of her. I was not granted sick leave. So, I quit my job. I did not sleep very well. I organised several fluorescent bulbs around Midori so that I could observe any minute change happening to her.

Late one night, I heard a drop. Waking up from my rare slumber, I saw that Midori had dropped her last remaining leaf. Enough is enough! I looked at Midori and shook her trunk with all my strength, screaming: 'Midori, Midori, what is happening to you?' I looked for clues and signs all over her bare, brown trunks and branches. Suddenly I saw pores, hundreds and thousands of them all over Midori. These were probably doors to get inside her. I wished I could walk in. But my human eyes were incapable of seeing what was really going on. My human body was too dense to enter through those pores.

There had been a lot of discussions lately about more than human lifeworlds and the technology of *species jump*. Pet owners paid a lot of money to get inside the consciousness of their pets, mainly to control their behaviour. The technology was illegal and did not receive formal government approval. I dived into the darknet and contacted a species jumper. He said that the technology worked for the human-to-animal species jumps. He knew only one person who had ever attempted a species jump into his houseplant, but that person never returned to tell the story. I said I did not care about the consequences and asked about the cost of a human-to-plant species jump.

'Lucky for you,' said the species jumper. 'There is currently a darknet call for experimental species jumpers. You could apply. Because of the failure of the last human-to-plant species jump, nobody responds to the call anymore. So, you might get the technology for free!'

I thanked him and logged off from the site to enter the designated darknet cell. I had to sign an informed consent that I was aware of the possibility of a permanent loss of my human consciousness. Then I had to drink 50ml of a bitter, green fluid named phytocommunicability spirit. It tasted like a spoiled herbal remedy. I had to attach a microchip under my skin and another chip on the main trunk of Midori. The local barbershop ran an illegal surgery room at the back for such procedures. It cost me a few hundred Euros, but I got the microchip sewn in. The third part of the procedure was simply annoying. I had to sit on the floor opposite Midori with closed eyes and breathe. For seconds, minutes, and hours. Nothing happened.

Suddenly I heard Midori's voice: 'You cannot just walk inside me. It is my place, my inner space. You cannot take over!' She sounded furious. I opened my eyes. All I saw was green. I tried to explain myself, but my mouth seemed to have dissolved into a semifluid mass. I heard Midori again: 'I do not need any explanation. Get out of my meristems! Right now!' I did not need to open my mouth. Midori heard all my thoughts. I thought: 'What is a meristem?' But then stopped asking intrusive questions. I apologised: 'I am sorry! I wished to help. I thought you were sick. I did not want to lose you.'

Midori continued with a wounded voice: 'Don't be so dramatic! I am not your grandfather. There is nothing wrong with me. This year the winter is unbearable, and so was your excessive curiosity about my people and me. So, I opted for the radical solution of dropping all my leaves. But before you decided to jump inside me, why did you not ask me for permission? You behave as if you care about me. You read up all about my family, genus, and the Latin names of my people! Did it ever occur to you that trying to *know* me and my people with intrusive methods was part of the reason why I lost all my leaves? I wished to send you a message that your extractivist expedition was not okay!'

I was too stunned to think. Midori continued.

'Why is it so important to *know* me, rather than learn to *live* with me? I am not that different from you. We are both multicellular beings. We share our breath. It is true that even as adults, my cells inhabit meristems, who continue to divide themselves and grow. The meristems produce specialised cells, cells of which you can only dream. We are much more superior than you humans. Do you realise that?'

I was speechless, vaguely remembering my botany classes in high school. The last thing I heard from Midori was: 'You have no business invading my consciousness! I do not need your help. You humans should rather help yourselves!'

I left Midori alone. As I receded from plant consciousness, Midori continued to expand and grow. Having lost my humanness, I was breathing and becoming Midori.

NARCISSUS

MARIA DONOVAN

Summer season in the packing shed. First Monday back. Familiar smells of flower bulbs and sandy soil, cardboard and concrete. It's three minutes to eight and the men are hanging round the end of their packing line, laughing about their holidays and eyeing/not eyeing the women in the queue for the clocking-in machine.

My turn at last. I reach for my card but it's not there. My heart skips. They knew I was starting today: I rang to make sure. Only the best of the best start so early in the season and I'm supposed to be one of them now. Not only that but there's the matter of obtaining a new work permit, which, ironically, I can only get if I have this job.

I glance over at the glass office. Derrick, our foreman, is leaning his knuckles on the Boss's desk, waiting for orders. I will have to go in there and muster my best Dutch, to say … what? '*Don't you want me?*'

Big Annie reaches round me and points to my card. It's moved down in alphabetical order, that's all. '*Thanks,*' I say and punch in. I'm so relieved, I'm grinning now and fumbling around in my head for some more words, but she strides ahead of me and into our packing shed with its long rows of tables. Her friend Corrie is already there. They have a permanent place in the nearest top corner with their backs to the window. They are the tallest women here with full control over the piece rate and the radio.

Here in the factory, flower bulbs come in at one end, where men guard them and keep them cool and quiet in special stores. Our shed is the heart of the building with great doors at either end: bulbs are brought in to us, and we count them into bags, pouches, and boxes that are loaded into wire-bottomed trays. The trays are stacked onto small pallets and when the stack is high enough, teenage boys cart them out to the men, who perform a kind of energetic dance along their packing line, unfolding big flat-packed cardboard boxes, sealing them, putting in a cardboard tray for strength, passing them along to be filled, closed, labelled, counted, and loaded on to big pallets ready to be forklifted out to the loading bay. Off they go for export, most of them to the UK. I could look for them in the shops back home except that 'home' has melted away now.

I move further in, nodding to anyone who looks at me. I'm wondering who is new, and who has pushed in ahead of me in alphabetical order. But I can only see the regulars, teamed up in pairs, ready for any of that better-paid, standing-up, four-handed work.

I'm on my own and don't know where I'm going, but I can smell the bulbs stacked in trays waiting to be deployed, and look for an empty table near the ones I like best: not the inevitable tulips (their acid eats under your fingernails), nor the hyacinths (blue, pink or white, their papery skins disintegrate into a horribly effective itching powder), not even anemones, bitty and scratchy, a sitting-down job and not very well paid. But here are the daffodil bulbs. Smooth and shiny. They cause some people skin irritation but so far they've done me no harm.

Except that I think of them as graveyard flowers. Every springtime a mass of green spears pushing up through the dark earth like an army rising. The flourish of trumpets white and yellow. Spring cheerful and faithful year after year – until they come up blind and have to be divided. I did that with my mum on Dad's grave the year before she died. She's buried there now, too.

I can't afford the tears that prickle in my eyes. I set my face hard, lean against the table and wait. The radio is sending out the eight o'clock news and my work time should begin. I study the bulbs. There isn't even a picture to show what they'll be like, but I imagine it will be a standard tall yellow daffodil. Bulbs leave here in their thousands and millions to be buried in foreign ground. Then up they come, growing wherever they are put.

I'm glad Mum chose something more unusual, paper-white narcissi with scented clusters of white heads, the stems not too tall, so as not to be blown down and look untidy, neat six-petalled flowers with modest white cups and bright orange centres.

In the springtime, as the fields here burst into colour, I took a trip back to Blighty, stayed in a B&B and visited the graveyard. It's near the place they moved to when they retired. It cheered me to see daffodils that other people had planted already up and nodding in the sunshine. But my parents' grave mound had been unexpectedly flattened and was still muddy, and the bulbs, inexpertly replanted, were struggling to grow. Some of them were too shallow and pushing out of the soil, others lying on their sides, twisting upwards towards the light. I went away more upset than I have been in a long time. Even now with no one to talk to, the words I want to say rattle and echo inside my own skull. I feel I have let my parents down and they aren't here to tell me that it's all right. For the umpteenth time I tell myself I ought to write a letter to someone at the graveyard and complain. At least make my voice heard.

It would have been easier if I hadn't been so alone. Last summer I was living in a tent on the workers' campsite. We were all crammed in together in what used to be a farmyard, but it was cheap and there were plenty of English speakers around. In the winter I'd been grateful for the warmth of a room in a house, though at first it seemed odd that the walls didn't move in the wind. Now here I am, already known to the tax man, and obliged to turn up at a police station at regular intervals to get a stamp in my passport. To be scrutinised and judged and made to wait to see if I'm acceptable.

In the shared house, I've tried to make friends but the others are suspicious or at least not interested. Anyway, they don't want to talk when I meet them in the kitchen. As the spring days lengthened I went out on long bike rides through the bulb fields, practising Dutch phrases. *How magnificent the tulips are!* Long swathes of colour. I even did the tourist thing of visiting a big show garden with all its fancy displays organised by the various bulb-growing firms: carefully assembled drifts through woodland, and all manner of playful and formal designs, using every variety of texture, colour and size, each flower growing alone but batched in groups with their own kind.

Some of the indoor display rooms were too crowded to get round and I picked up an information leaflet, which told me in five languages that millions of bulbs were planted in these gardens every year. I wanted to ask one of the stewards, '*What do you do with the bulbs at the end of the season?*' But I wasn't quite sure of the word order. Just then a young couple in warm coats and matching woolly hats, holding the same flier, asked more or less the same question. The steward said, '*We throw them all away.*'

We stood open-mouthed.

'*What?*' said the woman.

The man shook his head.

'*Can't you give them to people, or to some place that would like them, the garden of an old people's home or …*' said the woman.

I nodded and the woman caught my eye.

The steward said, '*We don't let the new bulbs develop. As soon as the garden is closed we dig everything out.*'

'*I wouldn't have come here if I'd known that,*' the woman said. '*What a waste.*'

'*It's all about the display of flowers,*' said the steward. '*All the energy goes into the bloom and not the bulb.*'

'*They could still let them grow!*'

'*They want to keep the goodness in the ground for next year's display. As soon as the plants are out they start building up the fertility.*'

When the couple moved on, looking as disgruntled as I felt with this state of things, I drifted out behind them in the hope that they would talk to me. But after all, what else was there to be said? And the thought that they might think I was hanging around them on purpose gripped my heart and in the end I scurried past them with no more than a tortured smile.

As I cycled back to my room, I thought at least the plants in the long wide bulb fields are allowed to reproduce. No chance of hybridisation, since the heads are all cut off before they can set seed. All the sun's energy must go into producing a good bulb to sell – and they grow copies of themselves, by the miracle of asexual reproduction.

I understand the commercial aspects of the business – the garden is a showcase, a way to build reputation. But whenever I think of those millions of plants thrown away, I feel uneasy.

The news is over and the music begins again, playing a cheerful old tune about waking up and feeling fine. Derrick, a short man in his middle years with a soft roundness to him that makes him seem cuddly, emerges from the Boss's office and comes straight towards me. I stop leaning and stand up straight and say, '*Good morning.*' But he only nods and inserts his little cart under a pallet to wheel a stack of daffodil bulbs away from me and over to the corner where Annie and Corrie are waiting to begin.

Once they are settled, he comes straight back to me, utters the magic word '*Narcissus*' and nods to the table. Relieved, I hastily arrange myself. I like to sit with my back to the wall. From here I can watch everyone else and see how fast they're going, keep my eye on the clock, and try to shave seconds off my time. If Corrie and Annie are packing the same as me it will be a good test. I set a small pallet on the floor beside me on my right-hand side and add an empty tray. After the first stack I'll know if this is the quickest side for filling. Derrick himself throws the first lot of slippery golden bulbs on to the table for me and opens the cardboard box filled with clean-smelling, long, slim, white paper bags stamped on the top flap with the single word 'Narcissus' upside down in green letters. 'Ten,' he says, spreading the short fingers of both hands. He doesn't speak good English and I know he's being friendly in making the effort. I smile and say '*Ten*,' in Dutch and he looks pleased that I'm making the effort, too.

In the very beginning, I had the feeling that Derrick did not like me much, that all of us foreign summer workers were a nuisance, a noisy unknown quantity. He relied on Ina the supervisor to talk to us in English. But he cheered up when he saw that I was doing my best to say the necessary words in Dutch (*More bulbs! Take away! Throw down!*) and when I escaped from hourly pay into the territory of piecework and garnered a reputation for being neat and quick, I began to receive a little more respect all round. First I matched myself against Carla and her mate (whose name I can't remember) and overtook them. Now Derrick goes to them, across the way from me in the middle row and they start groaning because he wants them to pack hyacinths. '*Not on the first day, Derrick!*' And '*But Derrick, we're wearing the wrong clothes.*'

'*Tomorrow,*' he tells them because he is, after all, not a monster. They puff out their cheeks because tomorrow, no matter how warm it is, they'll have to wear long sleeves and high necks, and scarves around their faces and even this won't keep out whatever it is in the shrunken remains of last year's bulb – the dry skins that cover the new bulb with a pearly sheen in blue or white or pink – whatever it is that makes you itch and burrows into your skin like scabies.

Carla and her mate can hardly complain when he gives them tulips instead but they look sulky as this puts them in the low-grade company of old ladies, school kids, and foreigners. They will regain their pride by racing each other and the clock.

All the women are settled to their work when there's a whistle from one of the men out on the packing line and three new girls come into our shed, all shy and clustered together, two of them twittering like sparrows and the third glancing around as if she's not sure this can be the right place.

All the women look at them with lopsided smiles: three pretty young girls with long unbound hair, wearing nice jeans and clean tops. They look about 15 and make me, at 22, feel very old. They have no clue that their clothes will soon be ruined by bulb dust, and worn threadbare from rubbing against the sides of the table.

Ina bustles over to greet them. It was Ina who said, at the end of my first summer season, when she knew I would come back: '*Congratulations. But now you must speak Dutch.*' Since then, I have been rather silent. I'm still working my way through a book optimistically called *Dutch in Three Months*. I listen and pick up what I can.

My table has three empty places and I brace myself for company but instead Ina settles the twitterers with Carla and her mate, and brings the other one over to me. She looks glum at being separated from the others.

There are formal introductions. Sometimes I forget to pay attention to people's names and this makes everything awkward, as with Carla's mate, but the girl's name is Hilda and this makes such a formidable impression on me that I know I will remember it. '*Welcome, Hilda,*' I say, though I don't stop packing for a moment. The girl takes a seat diagonally opposite me, as far away as she can get. She shakes back her long hair and sighs. Her cheeks are full and her plump neck has two deep horizontal creases in it as if someone has tried garrotting her recently with the thin gold chain she's wearing.

Ina shows her how many to put in the bag, how to fold the flap over and centre a staple under the green word Narcissus, then leaves her with me and goes back to check on the other two, reminding them that *they* are being paid by the hour and not to chat. Everyone starts off on minimum wage, which is just as well as some of the summer packers would earn very little if they had to rely on piecework.

Hilda takes a stack of the empty paper bags and smooths them out. Picks one up and opens it. Holds it open with one hand, counts bulbs into it with the other. I can see her lips moving. She drops a bulb, scrapes a nail, and stops to examine it, peers into the bag again because she's forgotten how many she's put in, empties it out and starts over. When the bag is full she looks around for her stapler. Holds the bag and the stapler horizontally trying to get one into the jaws of the other. '*No,*' I say. '*Look.*' I show her that it's best to keep the bottom of the bag on the table (unnecessary movements cost time) and bring the stapler down over the flap vertically. It makes it much easier to put the staple in the right place. '*It has to be horizontal,*' I tell her.

She nods and grimaces and carries on. She doesn't want me telling her anything and I'm not going to waste my time any more. Time is money to me. And being good at this is all I have. I speed up and my movements are fast and neat, and almost fierce. I am on my third tray before she has finished one.

'*You're being paid by the hour, I take it,*' I say to her.

She looks startled as if I have woken her from a reverie of some kind. I feel a little jealous that she's able to drift off.

I always thought I'd have plenty of time for higher thoughts, doing this job, but the rhythm of the process takes over, it gets into your head: the clicking, the counting, the quick glances at the clock. I envy her a little but at the same time I despise her. Perhaps I want her to pack bulbs in her sleep, as I will, and be tormented by seeing that word in green over and over and over in her dreams: *Narcissus, Narcissus, Narcissus.*

The mythology behind the word is not lost on me. Narcissus, who fell in love with his own reflection. And the daffodils too, will lean over the banks and look at themselves in the water. I wonder if it means anything to Hilda.

Ina works her way right round the room doing her checks before she comes to us again, but I notice she keeps glancing over. Perhaps she thinks I should be talking to Hilda more, putting her at ease, and helping her along. She's not someone I want to have as a partner when the total earnings are shared between two. Carla and her mate can match each other for speed, more or less, which saves bad feelings and resentment.

At last Ina comes back to us. She can tell by look and feel whether a closed packet holds nine or eleven instead of ten, and although I am careful, her scrutiny always makes me feel anxious. But she goes away satisfied.

I say to Hilda. '*She worries the Big Boss will come.*' Not the Boss in the office here, who is aloof, but the Big Boss who sweeps in with two or three others, gathering factory notables into his entourage as he goes round the tables. He makes a close inspection of the work right down to the neat positioning of staples.

It is an odd thing that he always speaks in English, as if he wants to show that *his* work is important, international, even though most people here are Dutch and sometimes have to struggle to find the right words to give him an answer. Last year a girl he was telling off for late arrival said between gritted teeth, 'I overslept my time,' while Ina looked off into the distance.

Hilda looks blankly at me. I think about explaining some more but instead I smile and set off on another race against the clock.

The news on the hour at ten signals the first official break. Hilda spends it with her mates at their table; some people go to the canteen. I drift to the loo and then out through the men's packing shed, which smells more of cardboard and less of dust, and is cooler than our shed, more pleasant in the heat with the big doors open. It's better for the bulbs that will be stored here waiting to go. If they're too warm they might think it's springtime and start sprouting. Each one holds inside its swollen shape the buds of next year's growth, the leaves and flowers hidden and secure within their portable food supply. They can be planted anywhere and something will appear. But still, they do better if fed, if planted in good soil. If years go by, the roots contract, pulling the bulbs deeper and deeper into the earth. But for now they are in their prime, counted and boxed, ready for transit. Soon the first lorry loads will leave here, never to return.

I just want fresh air and the sight of something green. Behind the factory is an apron of tarmac bordered by a bit of grass and the obligatory watery ditch. Shrubs of *Rosa rugosa* will keep people out but I find one small gap and look out over bulb fields stretching as far as a distant line of trees. The fields between, apart from some untidy stands of dahlia, are for the most part dull and empty now, grey-brown and already smelling of pig shit. Just the small battalions of dahlia, with their big flower heads, dark red, sunshine yellow and peachy pink, stand out against the dull outlook. A plane scars the blue sky with its own white trail. I wonder where it's going. And what about me? I didn't mean to get stuck here and yet this is all I have.

It isn't Hilda's fault she finds the work boring. It isn't her fault that I will never see 21 again, or that no one was with me to help make my birthday special. I celebrated on my own, but all the time I wanted to tell someone. The words were going round and round in my head.

I will try to be nice and speak to her in Dutch. Yes. I will try.

After the break the music sets us flying, the hands of time pulling us on to greater speeds. I'm still behind the pace set by Annie and Corrie and I take a minute to reassess my way of doing things. I play with the configuration of the objects in front of me. This task is not so complicated. Take a bag, count bulbs into it, fold over the flap, staple it shut, line the bags in a tray, in five lines of ten and stack the trays five high. Two hundred and fifty per stack. Standing up work is a bit faster because you can go eight high before you have to reset with a new pallet. The speed comes from cutting out unnecessary movement and from keeping both hands working. I have tried keeping the bag on the table and leaning it back against the raised side, copying Annie and Corrie. But that means taking each bag one by one and setting it in place. Now I think that if I have a whole sheaf of bags on my lap leaning against the outside edge of the table and snick the top one open with my left hand I can already be reaching for the first trio of bulbs with my right.

Hilda looks miserable and I say to her, '*Would you like me to show you how to go faster? It's more fun and you can earn good money.*' It even seems to me sometimes that this economy of movement can be applied to life, and that a sense of order can do much to soothe a troubled soul. At the very least it is a puzzle and a challenge and some kind of race.

Hilda seems uninterested. I try again. '*I'm English. I don't speak Dutch very good yet …*'

'Oh but we can speak English!' she says, her face lighting up.

I get this all the time. I go into the bakers with my carefully rehearsed '*Half a sliced brown please*' and back comes 'One twenty. Anything else?'

'*No thank you*,' is my usual answer. I might be seething but the only way forward is to be persistent. I will batter them with their language until they stop trying to speak mine.

It is not just that I want to be good at Dutch, I am also afraid that my way of speaking and thinking in English will be contaminated by such charming mistakes as TV hosts make when they say things like 'Welcome in the show!'

'*I want to learn to speak Dutch,*' I say.

'Oh,' says Hilda. 'Me too. But it's so difficult isn't it? Really, English is my first language. I grew up in Canada.'

A feeling of unease spreads through me. I say, straight out, 'Are you related to the Big Boss?'

'Yes.' She is a little shamefaced. 'He's my uncle. I'm just here on holiday.'

I nod. A Dutch person would have said something like 'I'm on my holidays'.

Ina is frowning at us. I hope Hilda will not repeat what I said about her.

'Is he coming in?' I ask.

'Tomorrow?' She offers this with an apologetic shrug.

I suggest to Hilda that since we are both learning Dutch, we should try to speak it to each other. We swap small phrases interspersed with explanations and comments in English and carry on in this comfortable way until lunchtime.

In the loos I see Annie and say casually, '*I hear the Big Boss is coming in tomorrow.*'

'*Ah*,' she says.

In the early afternoon, as Derrick comes to take Annie's stack I see her mouth is telling him something.

I finish my stack soon after. Derrick adds 250 to the tally on my scrap of card with a jaunty flourish and a 'sank you very mush.' Hilda and I both titter.

The afternoon music is softer, the low rumble of bulbs rolling over tables soothes me and I'm already looking forward to the bike ride home and giving my legs some exercise. Hilda is copying me now and getting quicker. We work without much talking and I must have drifted into a kind of reverie after all, because it is nearly tea break time before I look around me and see that I'm dangerously ahead of the rate. Half a stack ahead of Corrie and Annie, who keep glancing over. Ina is frowning again. As Derrick goes by he chews the inside of his cheek.

I rub my arms and shoulders and take a break. Sometimes I wish I had not given up smoking because people are allowed to slope off outside for five minutes in their own time if they are drawn there by addiction. I could say I need some air but I don't move.

If the price goes down a cent per bag everyone will hate me. I shudder, despite the heat. Hilda, seeing me pause, stops too and gets out her phone. I never touch mine while I'm at work because of the dust, though I keep it in my bag, wrapped in plastic, in case of an emergency.

I start again but take my time so that the others can catch up.

'You're so quick,' she says, sighing. 'I'll never be able to do that.'

'*You could*,' I say. '*If you wanted to.*' I'm glad she told me about her uncle. I could so easily have confided in her that I've been going too fast.

'The trouble is,' she says, 'I don't. Not really. It's so boring. A machine could do it.'

'*There are machines next door*,' I snap. '*Maybe you must work in there.*' It's the worst job in the factory, stuck in an inner room with only very high windows. Bulbs go into a big hopper, two people sit opposite each other holding a bag under a chute and passing them to two others, who staple them shut. You can't stop unless the machine stops. No counting to do, no control over the rhythm. You are just part of the machine. And the people talk and talk and talk. I was in there for a while last year with an Englishwoman who never stopped and if you didn't listen, if you didn't keep up with her stories, she got angry. She didn't want you to say anything but she wanted your attention.

I had gathered up all the Dutch I had been practising and asked Derrick, '*Please can I come back?*'

He agreed and I set about making myself indispensable.

I can't go back in there.

Just after tea break there's a bustle and the Big Boss comes in. His unexpected appearance gives everyone a shock and the rhythm falters, while the music plays on. As he checks our table, with Ina right behind him, he talks to his niece in English as if he doesn't recognise her. He looks at the scrap of card that shows her tally and then he looks at mine. 'Why have you done less,' he says to her, 'when she has done more?' I feel the jaws of danger opening again.

'*I'm new here,*' she says, with a smile. '*I'm learning.*'

'Huh,' he says and sweeps away to bother someone else.

The next morning I cycle to work and I am almost looking forward to talking to Hilda again. For her this is only a holiday job, but maybe she will see the value in becoming fast and we'll be a good team.

Her friends arrive, but Hilda doesn't turn up at my table. Perhaps she's asked to work on one of the machines. At break time, she doesn't appear. I saunter over to talk to the two girls, who are both wearing rubber gloves today.

'*Where is Hilda today?*'

'She iss not here,' says one.

'She het a ferry bet reaction to ze bulps,' says the other.

'*Pity*,' I say. '*Tulips are usually the worst. Apart from hyacinths.*'

They both look glum.

I could tell them that wearing gloves will make no difference. Somehow the acid gets through or the dust gets inside and the heat and sweat make the pain worse. And the gloves slow you down. But it's only a few weeks of torture for them and they will find out for themselves.

ROCK SAMPHIRE, *Crithmum maritimum*

A CLEAR VIEW

MARK BOWERS

Poor John Smith. When I first met him, he was in a difficult place, as precarious but indomitable as greenery clinging to an inhospitable rock face. His responsibilities and relationships stressed him out and compounded general anxieties that he couldn't quite put a finger on. These threats to his well-being had begun, he believed, in utero. His maternal grandmother had died three months prior to his birth, an episode from which his mother struggled to recover. His brother, older by five years, resented his arrival and teased him spitefully during childhood by insisting that he was adopted, while his father found the attraction of a busy job useful in order to avoid the domestic setting.

Angry and anxious behaviours were recognisable in each family member, but were for some reason always associated specifically with John. This resulted, John said, with him harbouring a persistent feeling of guilt. His parents did little, he claimed, to remedy his lack of self-worth. Consequently, he often found himself testing them with bad behaviours, seeing how far he could go, how far he could push them. By removing himself he could avoid the downward spiral that they provoked.

He moved east. To Kent. Towards the rising sun, hopeful of a fresh start.

'Families are the most beautiful thing in the world.' That is a line from my favourite book, Louisa May Alcott's *Little Women*, and these words often bubble up into my thoughts when I ponder John Smith and the experiences of his early years.

I had known him intimately, and although changeable and occasionally melancholic, he was a good friend. If you wanted a bosom buddy, he was your man. When he felt thwarted by his upbringing, he would tell me about it and occasionally it occurred to me that he may be unable to cope and was about to plummet into some bottomless chasm like the one in Dante's *Inferno*. Like Dante, John could be a bit dramatic. He even once remarked, 'When will I emerge from this purgatory?'

Yes, he loved his drama. I adopted the view that he possessed a strong affiliation with his family, but enjoyed a safer, more stable existence when living apart from them. Like Dante, he was an exile.

When I relocated temporarily to my home town in the state of Wyoming, John and I maintained contact by telephone. He gave me the impression of being grounded, and I treasured each moment with him during my visits to the UK. My heart raced in anticipation of each meeting, like the moment one spots a thriving spread of rock samphire while foraging, its thick, luminous green and fleshy fingers rising up from some precarious fissure in a desert of chalk and flint. The domes of green flowers are humble. I can almost hear them say, 'Oh, we are most honoured, ma'am, that you should enjoy us, salty and unsophisticated as we are.' John welcomed me into his life in much the same way, and it was an easy decision to return to Kent and settle down there.

I first met him below Shakespeare Cliff near Dover, when he asked, 'What are you doing down here?'

'Isn't it obvious?' I hadn't meant to sound obtuse; it just came out that way. It wasn't as if my purpose was concealed or mysterious. My basket was stacked tall with stems of a pea-green shade going on lime. Feeling more conciliatory, I continued, 'I'm collecting samphire, for cooking. This type only grows on the edge of chalk cliffs.'

He accepted my response with a nod, then asked me the question so many Brits ask, 'Are you American?'

'Yes, from Hope Springs.'

'That sounds positive!'

I laughed. 'It's in Wyoming. Why are you down here?'

He hesitated, then confided, 'It reminds me of home.'

'And where is that?'

'Stone Cross.'

'That sounds kinda grumpy!'

As he laughed, I saw his frame relax. 'It's in East Sussex, near a place with colossal chalk cliffs called Beachy Head. It is the reason I come here, now I'm living in Kent. I love the light, the smells, the soft-white chalk. It's *so* like Beachy Head, and I suppose that the familiarity is reassuring, a consolation of sorts. The sky, the sea, the pure pale cliffs. Walking here clears my mind.'

His laugh resembled the stuttering voices of the jackdaws as they tumbled at the cliff edge with closed wings, then stretched to glide on warm air like kites on a string. John told me that Shakespeare mentions samphire in his great tragedy, *King Lear*.

'I played Cordelia in a school production, but I don't recall a samphire reference. To me it was just a sad story with a sad ending.'

That night, as I cooked him lemon sole with samphire, he recited the harrowing Heath scene from *King Lear*, 'Blow, winds, and crack your cheeks! Rage! Blow! ...'

His dramatic skills were accomplished, and I was captivated initially until it became hard going. King Lear was clearly a man with issues. John did his best but the lengthy recitation took its toll, I could tell. He broke off with the words, '… man's nature cannot carry. The affliction nor the fear.' John stared at the carpet for a bit, chin on chest. The air felt heavy. I gave a sideways glance and saw John's head roll back. The sudden sound of his voice made me jump. 'That speech was made by a broken and distraught Lear who, it could be said, hit rock bottom on that cliff, the cliff where we met today, which is why it is now known as Shakespeare Cliff.'

I knew this of course, having played Cordelia, but I let him talk. It wasn't all doom and gloom. The evening picked up a bit after that. I gave him some encouragement and we fell into bed. After that, John and I were an item for a while.

My foraging for samphire was still a novelty the day I met John. While we remained together, we associated it with our chance meeting. Once, rosy-cheeked and limb-heavy after walking above the crashing waves near Mousehole in Cornwall, we collapsed in our B&B as the last rays of sun warmed the bedroom. I held his hand as we stared at the ceiling. 'What compelled you to collect samphire that day?' John asked.

'A desire for sustenance. Hunger. Isn't that what drives us all? To do is to be. I forage therefore I am.'

He sat up and, as he held a direct stare for some time, my scalp prickled and a sudden discomfort weighed me down. What did he want to hear? That I was hunting a husband? That I'd followed him in order to speak to him? The words fell slowly from his lips with the same slow, sonorous burble as the incoming tide among rocks.

'Your choice to visit the foreshore was a risky decision. Instead of meeting me, you might have slipped and cracked your skull, been crushed by a rock-fall, or swept out to sea by a rogue wave.'

Maybe he was trying to say he cared about me. The John I knew had an interest in existential philosophy, and the theories of Kierkegaard and Camus intrigued him. He was occupied by questions of life and its meaning and enjoyed discussing the lived experience in these terms. I recall John as a man determined to reveal how a meaningless world affected the individual. Before a day trip to London one dull fall day, he decided he wasn't going.

'But we've planned this for ages.'

'Let's face it, we'll be plodding along packed, wet streets breathing exhaust fumes. Why? What for?'

I bit my tongue. I didn't say it. I didn't want to demean him, but then I said it anyway, 'I remember an occasion when Bertie Wooster said he was frustrated at being unable to make up his mind what to do and Jeeves said that Hamlet also dithered. I'm all for doing, not dithering, John. Get your shoes on.'

John smiled, eventually, and said, 'We are all of us the product of experience. Our freedom to make choices in this world determines those experiences. It is humanity's great limitation. We are lame but limp on, even though the freedom to choose results in this impediment found within us all: anxiety. A great deal rests on our decisions, and a lot can go wrong. Hence the angst. Hence the horror of our existence.'

I listened respectfully, but I wanted to say, 'My observation is that while life throws up experiences that get in the way, we just get on with it, don't we?'

Our visit to London was affected by the heavy rain and another tiff we had on the way.

Crithmum maritimum, commonly known as rock samphire, exists at that harsh and exposed boundary where land, sea, and sky meet. Towering cliffs and rocky foreshore offer a feeble cradle to its fleshy form. It resists the salt of the tide, tolerates the desert of chalk and rock, and drinks from the moist air. In Nelson's day, it was stowed in barrels of brine to combat scurvy aboard the creaking ships-of-the-line. No doubt its dietary benefits were discovered by association, as a citrus taste invades the tongue when the leaves are chewed. Nelson even mentioned rock samphire while aboard HMS *Theseus*, the victor's vessel at the Battle of the Nile: 'No captain can do wrong that ships samphire.' Perhaps he meant that Jack Tar, the British matelot, can withstand any threat if fed on it. I wonder if Nelson was aware that his ship's namesake, Theseus, was fed samphire prior to slaying the Minotaur?

Rock samphire is often mistaken for the unrelated *Salicornia europea*, the marsh samphire, an imposter that inhabits tidal flats and creeks, a wimp that cannot survive on rugged shores. How appropriate that marsh samphire is known to many as glasswort, suggesting something easily fractured. This fragile sham can fool the uninitiated when sent to the table as a complement to lemon sole. Be warned; send it back, you are being short-changed. Don't accept second best. *Crithmum maritimum* is the true queen of all sea succulents. Those who study word lore suggest that samphire derives from the French and is a corruption of Saint Pierre. That would be appropriate. St Peter the Rock. Rock samphire. It all dovetails.

The classification of plants helps us make sense of the world around us. Belonging to the family *Apiaceae*, which includes fragrant plants such as carrot, coriander, and hemlock, *Crithmum maritimum* is designated by biologists as a sole species, so unique and alone it is called monospecific. To my way of thinking this indicates that rock samphire has no brothers and sisters, and that the carrot, coriander, and hemlock are merely distant, unacquainted cousins.

As the years multiplied, John and I saw each other less frequently. When he was down my way he would pop by, so I guess he visited me as much as he visited his own family. John was discovered walking close to the cliff edge at Beachy Head in East Sussex late one evening in November. He was encouraged to talk about his presence there by a trained counsellor, part of a team that regularly patrols that ill-famed precipice. When John spoke to me about this, he framed it as an opportunity for research.

'We spoke at length,' John recalled, 'and the counsellor was encyclopaedic. After some time spent appraising the ways in which a mental crisis might become apparent to others, she said, "Are you feeling any pain?" In the context of our conversation her question was sensitively put. I told her that I experienced anxiety like anyone, and difficulty in maintaining relationships too. That gave her the opportunity to give, rather than pose another question. "Yes, relationships can be demanding to maintain, but we are social animals. So we need to keep talking, keep making choices."'

As a cloud covered the moon, John could no longer see her face. He told her that he thought that this was a place to come to make choices. Some that came here chose to end their lives, but it was not an impulsive act. She was silent and stopped walking. The chalk path where she stood was just discernible in the darkness, a white line coursing through the grass and clover worn into the ground by those who had walked this path before. Her voice was quite clear and steady.

'It is never too late to review a choice. We are all of us searching. Whatever brings someone to this location, it is a temporary urge. Talking can help. A fresh perspective on the pain or emotions that prompt their decisions can affect the choices they make.'

The counsellor stayed there, in the black air. A warm wind battered John's back as he faced her. The cliff edge was some way distant behind him now as the path had taken them away from the edge. At that moment, John said that I popped into his head. He thought of me foraging for samphire and that the foreshore below Beachy Head would be the sort of place he might find me. If he were looking for me. He told the woman that he ought to be getting back and thanked her for talking. She walked part of the way with him.

John looked me in the eye. 'I bet she thinks she saved a life that night.' Then he winked and said that he had selected Beachy Head as a site to ponder existential theory. Specifically, he wished to think about something Albert Camus had written. John often walked when he was figuring something out, exactly as he was the day I met him at Shakespeare Cliff. His family had been preying on his mind, and John said the patrolling volunteer on Beachy Head gave him the freedom to consider without constraint what that French philosopher had said, a woman devoted to deterring the melancholic and the heartbroken from their darkly chosen path, beside a cliff edge, five hundred feet above the rocky shore. He emphasised the absurdity of his situation close to the void on that dark fall night. The amateur philosopher searching for the meaning of life, while being counselled by a stranger on the edge of a notorious abyss. East Sussex being the county of his childhood, he took the opportunity to visit his ageing mother the following day.

John and I lost touch over time. The last time I saw him he praised my laughing spirit and said it was an excellent thing. Head-hunted, he departed for an academic role in a Scottish university and left me like *Crithmum maritimum*. Monospecific. Alone.

Looking back, I find myself unconvinced by John's claim that life revolves around the freedom to choose and the anxiety it provokes. No, I think it's about family and friendship. *That* is the beauty of life. I should know, having never been part of a family. The closest I ever got was the community of the Sweetwater Mercy Children's Home in Hope Springs, Wyoming. Without the amity John provided, I sometimes lose my way. However, here in East Sussex, from this high vantage point, I can see clearly, and the seascape vista is breathtaking.

The bitter smell of rock samphire can repel, so cooks recommend boiling it or frying it in butter. I wash it and use it raw to preserve the fresh citrus flavour. That sharp, salty tang on my tongue always feels like a sunrise, like a fresh tide coming in.

There are stairs at Beachy Head now. They were installed to allow tourists and beachcombers easy access to the foreshore, offering a gentle descent among like-minded others compelled to experience the junction of sky, land, and sea: raw, fresh elements offering a new beginning.

NIGELLA

THALIA HENRY

The salty air is bright and crisp as it sweeps across Tilly's face through the open kitchen windows of Mr Collier's cul-de-sac house in Karitane, New Zealand. Tilly sweeps and dusts, vacuums and polishes, mops and takes out the compost, all the while alternating between whistling and humming. She's fit from the cleaning jobs that she does around the community – for the elderly, or those who run B&Bs – and since there are possibly more baches (holiday houses) than homes in the village, just a short drive away from the city of Dunedin, she's never short of work. She pauses as she drops the compost and looks over the paddock that sweeps behind Mr Collier's house beyond to the view of Huriawa, the peninsula home of two breathing blowholes. She might take her camera there later, see if she can capture the play of shadow that hits the steep sides. Once, the story goes, two lovers fell to the stones chattering beneath bubbling water whooshing in and out below.

When she returns to the kitchen, Tilly looks around. She's nearly finished her cleaning routine, but she'll give the sills a wipe. She runs a cloth beneath the kitchen tap. In two jars above the sink sit cuttings of a plant. Tilly studies the image as if capturing it through a camera lens frame. Inside each jar, Mr Collier has positioned bulb-shaped cuttings that look like some sort of spiky seed pods. They're not cactuses, because it's clear they're hollow inside, but the pods appear resilient like cactuses do. The two jars are different sizes and shapes, refracting light. The larger of the two on the left is square, tinged green where its walls meet, while the smaller jar is a tube shape with a wide neck about a third of the size. The bulb in the square jar is green, as if plucked from his garden only yesterday, or this morning, and the pair on the right are brown. Around the seed pods and spreading along the stalks are curved spikes, the outlines in sharp relief against the window, blurred with dust, rendering the trees behind it unfocussed, too. The last time that Tilly had cleaned the kitchen, and the time before that, she recalls only the brown pods on the sill. Why had Mr Collier chosen these cuttings, she wonders – such otherworldly-looking things?

Mr Collier is in his bedroom having his afternoon nap. Tilly doesn't know how old he is, but he must be her oldest client. When she arrived at his home for the first time, it amazed her how tidy the place was, and when he'd said that he hadn't received any home help before, she assumed this meant nursing care, too. He certainly looked ancient – when she met his gaze, his pupils seemed to float a little as if unattached in their irises of pale water.

That evening, Tilly walks along the path leading up the peninsula. She takes some pictures by the blowholes even though the light isn't sitting at the angle she'd imagined. The act of taking pictures is half-hearted too because through the lens, she's still visualising the seedpods in the jars. She's seen that sort of plant before, somewhere, though she can't call the place to mind. She closes her eyes and the curved spikes emerging from the seedpods seem to reach out and twist.

A seagull caws. Tilly opens her eyes and studies the tussock around her feet – the spokes splay evenly, and not in all directions like those emerging from the seed pods.

It isn't until Tilly returns home, and is about to fall asleep, thinking of not much at all, that she remembers where she's seen the pods before. There's a watercolour picture on Mr Collier's hallway wall. He's hung a lot of pictures around his home, so it isn't too surprising that she didn't pay close attention.

The following week, Tilly calls Mr Collier and asks if she can come to clean an hour earlier so that she can wash the windows, too. She doesn't mention any extra charge because the job won't feel complete if she hasn't washed the windows and he's on a pension anyway, so she doesn't mind.

Tilly cleans the outside of the windows first. It seems more satisfying somehow, because when she moves inside and wipes, each pane will be as clear as she can get it. In the hallway with the bottle of cleaner hanging from her hand, Tilly pauses to study the watercolour image. In a blue ceramic jar, a collection of matching-coloured blue flowers splay out among the pods. The colours and tendrils stretch in all directions across a white background, but at the base of the painting a few strokes of blue signal a surface that the jar sits on. Tilly looks at one of the seed pods up close, at the delicate watercolour shading surrounded by inky lines. In a lilac frame, beneath the picture is scrawled the word *Nigella*, and beneath that, in the same italic handwriting, *Ada Collier*.

'My wife painted that.'

Tilly startles. Mr Collier is standing beside her. He must've been tall and broad-shouldered when he was a younger man.

'Nigella is so ugly that it's beautiful, don't you think?'

She nods and turns to Mr Collier, but his watery eyes are looking at the painting. He's leaning his weight onto his walking stick, but it doesn't look like he needs its support.

'Ada was, among her many talents, an art teacher.'

Tilly is still holding the bottle of glass cleaner. 'Would you like me to clean the pane?'

Mr Collier shakes his head. 'How about a cuppa instead?'

He shuffles into the kitchen and Tilly follows. Without asking what she'd like, he makes a pot of Earl Grey and beckons for her to sit. Tilly can't think of what to say even though she's usually good at making small talk with her clients. She'd like to ask questions about his wife but that wouldn't be appropriate, and she wonders how long he's lived alone. Tilly takes a sip of her tea. 'Are the seed pods a sort of Christmas decoration?'

He seems to consider this. 'It was around this time last year that I picked the brown ones. Of course, they weren't brown then. There's a nice sense of renewal with the two different-coloured seed pods side by side. All life gone from one. The other soon to turn the same colour.'

Tilly remembers seeing a faded picture of Ada in the lounge. 'They're not a regular sort of arrangement.'

'No, I guess not,' he pauses. 'Is your tea too hot? We could take a look at the nigella outside.'

He's standing up without waiting for a response. Mr Collier is so lithe for someone of his age, Tilly thinks, and more talkative than she'd thought he would be. This must be because she's arrived an hour earlier than usual before he retires for his nap. He opens the two French doors onto the porch and leads her down some stairs and around by the side of the house. Mr Collier rests his walking stick against an outside table so that his hand is free to hold the hand railing, but his steps aren't slow.

The nigella plant isn't as she'd imagined it would look. She reaches forward to touch it and then wonders if that's a presumptuous thing to do. Surprisingly, the spikes splaying in all directions have a softness to them and, unlike in the watercolour and in the jars on his sill, the seed pods have turned blue. They're surrounded by blue and white flowers that are larger than the pods. The plant doesn't look like a cactus at all anymore.

When Mr Collier reaches forward to brush the plant with his hand, his skin looks too thin, as if it's been stretched. 'The nigella plant produces black cumin seeds, but that isn't the only reason why I am fascinated by this plant. Don't you think that the *Nigella sativa* pods look like hearts, with arteries?' Mr Collier pauses. 'I was a doctor, you see. A heart surgeon. It interests me how nature replicates itself in surprising ways. I mentioned that to Ada once, and a few days later she arrived home with the watercolour. How she fitted that in among teaching her classes of teenagers, I've no idea. Maybe in her lunch breaks.'

Mr Collier falls quiet.

That evening, Tilly pulls up a chair at the kitchen table and opens her laptop. She lives in a rented cottage with just one flatmate who's hardly ever home, and this evening she's glad of the privacy. Night has fallen around her, but the light of the moon is bright. She Googles 'black cumin seeds' and reads about the antioxidant properties of the seed from the *Nigella sativa* plant, a species of buttercup. The antioxidants, she learns, may even help with heart disease. Could that have been why Mr Collier planted the nigella? Or had his wife planted it? Or perhaps neither had planted the nigella at all, and it had been at the residence before they had. It is likely that the elderly man is asleep by now. His window might be slightly ajar, the summer sea air cooling the room, the sound of the waves crashing at the beach the backdrop to his slumber. Tilly closes her eyes, too. She thinks of Mr Collier's heart like an enlarged nigella seed pod, pulsing slowly, breathing in and out as seawater bubbles through blowholes.

Tilly wakes up a few hours later in the chair. The position of the moon has moved and she's sore from having slept in a slumped position. Something feels different. Tilly shakes the unsettled feeling away and goes to bed. It isn't like her to think about the people that she cleans for so much, but she can't help but think of Mr Collier and the life that he's led. The nigella seedpods on his sill will be cast in darkness now, the opalescent moon glinting through the thin skin of the pods. The next time she visits, he'll very likely be napping and she won't be able to talk to him until it's time to clean his windows again. Next time, he mightn't be so forthcoming.

In the morning, Tilly goes to the shop to collect the paper and some milk. Over the last few days, the shop owner has taken to wearing long, feather-shaped rubber earrings. She's talking with another local, Mrs Jamieson. 'Oh, it's horrible, isn't it? To think that his grandson visited just this morning from Dunedin only to find that he'd passed in his sleep.'

'News spreads quickly in this town.'

'Oh, it does. It does. But it's hard to avoid overhearing when the young man has left his cellphone at home by mistake and comes into the shop to use the phone. His face was pale as a sheet.'

'So do you know if the body has been collected?'

'I don't think so. Not just yet. In fact, I know it hasn't. I'd have seen an ambulance go by. And then there'll be the whole process of the family needing to come to clear the house. It's dreadful. Dreadful.'

Tilly pops some coins on the bench for the paper and the milk. She doesn't need the change. A lot of elderly live in the village, so very occasionally someone passes away. That's the cycle of life – like the nigella cuttings side by side. She had brought her Keep Cup with her, thinking to treat herself to a coffee, but she chooses not to hang around.

A couple of days later and while Tilly's eating her Weet-Bix, her phone rings. It's probably her mother, who often calls in the morning before heading out to run errands. Tilly doesn't recognise the voice on the end of the line, and she lowers her spoon mid-air.

'Hello. My name is Thomas. I found your name in my grandfather's list of contacts.'

The voice sounds strange, higher pitched than a male's usually sounds, and it's as if the sentences are rehearsed.

'He has a phonebook that he keeps by the landline, so I'm just working through the process of calling around. I suppose you've heard that he has passed away.'

'Sorry, who?'

'Ern.'

'Perhaps you've got the wrong number. I don't know a man named Ern.'

'Mr Collier.'

The spoon drops from her fingers as splatters of Weet-Bix and milk splash on the tablecloth. It can't be so. Tilly saw Mr Collier just recently; he was moving freely, talking so lucidly about the *Nigella sativa* – the nigella seed pods that look like little hearts.

'My grandfather was 89, a ripe age, but he was independent, so it came as a shock. I'm glad at least that he's passed peacefully. That's what we all wish for ourselves.'

Tilly stammers. 'I'm sorry.'

There's a weighted pause at the end of the line followed by a tumble of words. 'Listen, the reason that I'm calling is that I know you did some cleaning for my grandfather. I was wondering if perhaps you could help with putting some things in boxes for the Salvation Army, or the tip, and help to clean the place. After the funeral that is, and I'd pay you of course. I hope you understand. Most of the immediate family lives in Christchurch and so I feel a sense of responsibility to organise as much as I can before they arrive. My mum, his daughter, particularly; she's too upset, and I just want to make sure that she doesn't have to do much besides grieve.'

'Of course.'

'You'll help?'

'Yes.'

Tilly can't recall the rest of the conversation but now the line is quiet. The grandson must have hung up.

A few days later, Tilly attends the funeral in Dunedin. It's cold and the air outside the funeral building window is drizzly and grey. She sits at the rear of the crowd with her hands crossed, her fingers latched together. Mr Collier's grandson speaks. He's tall with broad shoulders. Tilly hasn't introduced herself – she'll meet him soon, and he'll have many friends and family to talk to today. She won't stay for the after-service refreshments. A lady sitting at the front, who must be Mr Collier's daughter, weeps, and the coffin in the centre of the room, laden with flowers, looks too small, as if now that Mr Collier has passed, his body has reduced in size. Tilly can't help but stare at it and wonder whether perhaps she shouldn't have come after all.

'My grandad's life changed after he discovered that my grandmother, Ada, had passed away in the garden behind the house. For those who didn't know the couple then, she died of heart failure. It was a cruel turn of fate for a man who worked tirelessly to help others with heart problems ...'

Tilly clenches her eyes shut. How long would it take for the green nigella seedpod on Mr Collier's kitchen sill to turn brown like the pair beside it? Leaves take a while to turn to skeletons, so it might take a few months, or weeks at least. In her memory, she follows Mr Collier outside to the garden behind the house. The nigella was soft. She imagines Ada's head resting on it, cushioned by the flowers. The sky around her is blue and bright and clear and when Ern discovers her and picks her up, cradling her, the plant bounces back, resilient.

Tilly takes a deep breath before she opens the door to Mr Collier's house. Thomas hasn't arrived yet and for some reason, when she thinks of him, her pulse quickens. The house seems just the same. It's as if Mr Collier is asleep in his bedroom, enjoying his afternoon nap. His walking stick rests by his door. In the hallway, Tilly passes the watercolour. She makes her way to the kitchen where the cuttings in the jars sit side by side. The seedpod on the left is still green. A waxy, new growth green. Tilly takes her camera out of her backpack and positions her eye through the site. She pauses a moment before taking a single shot. Then, she opens the French doors, lets in some air, and walks down the steps to the garden to collect a sprig of her own.

A HOMESICK GHOST PRINCESS VISITS HER HOME ON A FULL MOON NIGHT

PRIYANKA SACHETI

Soon after becoming a ghost, the ghost princess realised this vital truth: all those rules of time and decorum that had once corseted her as a human being no longer applied. For instance, if she wished, she could arrive at the same place at the same time day after day, like a song played on loop. And if she desired to visit her home on a full moon night – she still thought of it as her home after all these years – she would just have to *appear* there. She would not have to announce her arrival in advance: all she had to do was glide through the wrought-iron gates and into the garden. She would then slip inside the shadow of her favourite tree, a friendly, ancient, spreading banyan, which had been there long before her and still stood sentinel after all these years, and watch the moon rise before it got entangled in the tree branches. It reminded her of a pearl earring she had lost decades ago – and even though she had lost so much else and of greater significance since then, the loneliness of that single pearl earring continued to haunt her.

And yet, over the years, the ghost princess started to question what she had once taken for granted as a newly minted ghost: could she *truly* arrive at her home whenever she pleased? In the absence of an heir, the government had taken over her house and converted it into a museum after she was no longer alive (she still could not bring herself to believe she was that ugly, final word: *dead*). In the beginning, though, she had been incensed at the thought of all those strange people pouring into and invading the precious, sacred privacy of her home. She had been a recluse for the last years of her life, becoming accustomed to the heavy silences that carpeted the rooms. The unceasing laughter and chatter that now filled the corridors unsettled her: she thought her ears and head would explode from the clamour. She resented the visitors examining her sarees or peering at their reflections in her silver hairbrushes or photographing the balcony where she had once taken her morning and evening tea till the very end.

Yet, over the passage of time, she began to see the house had now come alive, wonderfully so, glowing softly, deeply, as if it had fallen in love. She gradually accepted that the house was no longer the tomb it had been while she had called it home. Its mistress may have gone but the house had in turn acquired life – and how could she possibly begrudge it that? And with that realisation, she decided she would no longer venture inside anymore, limiting her explorations only to the garden.

It was a full moon tonight: her favourite time of the month. When she glided through the gates and into the garden, she saw that visitors were still walking around the place although the sun had long begun its descent. Newly in love couples whispered into each other's hair while two middle-aged women sat and gossiped on a stone bench. She made herself comfortable inside her favourite spot, the many-limbed banyan tree, her attention now drawn towards a skinny girl with huge black glasses intently photographing an enormous dawn-hued hibiscus bush. Even though the light was fading rapidly, its blooms still appeared so brilliant, their colour competing with the tangerine-pink sky. The princess personally did not like that hibiscus variety, which had always been a little too vulgar for her taste. She preferred their daintier candy-floss pink cousins, secretly seeing them as self-portraits. One of the gardeners had insisted on planting those huge hibiscuses and she had been surprised to see how soon they became the garden's star attractions, with everyone flocking to admire them. She too eventually became used to their flamboyant presence, although she still gravitated towards the pink hibiscus, the only ones that were permitted to adorn her hair and home.

The girl's eyes and camera were trying to capture the hibiscus, almost as if it were a rare butterfly. The girl eventually prised her gaze away from the flowers, perhaps conceding to the approaching darkness, and then glanced at the banyan tree. The princess shivered, terrified that the girl might have seen her. In the past, someone had once spotted and photographed her, sending the photographs to a local newspaper. There had then followed feverish speculation in the city for months, with everyone wondering about the identity of the shadowy figure in the images. A local historian gave a detailed interview to a TV channel, suggesting that the figure haunting the place was the house's former inhabitant, a princess from a faraway land. Thanks to his careless words, the home soon became overrun with people trying to get a glimpse of this mysterious ghost princess.

More guards than ever were deployed to ward off these amateur ghost hunters, whose numbers increased with each day. Is this how tigers or lions felt upon encountering humans during safaris, the ghost princess had wondered at the time?

She could not return to her beloved home for months and it was only after the furore finally died down that she dared to come back, making sure it was always after dusk and limiting her visits to every few days. Perhaps, it was then she had begun to realise that ghosts did have boundaries, after all, that they too could become trespassers in what had been their own homes. They ultimately had no choice but to follow a ghostly version of visitors' rules, adhering to a set of visiting hours and being permitted access only to certain spaces.

The girl stared at the tree for a minute before walking away – and the princess then sighed a breath of deep relief. The place soon emptied of people, for *their* visiting hours were now over, and the house was left to itself – and her. The night guards retreated into the little white gatehouse after bolting the gates shut. As the sky darkened to sapphire and the moon rose higher in the sky, she emerged from the shadows to claim what was once her own.

She began walking around the garden, pausing to inspect the lily pond that she had had made soon after moving into the house. The pale mauve, sun-hearted waterlilies were hiding under a thick coverlet of jade-hued leaves and their unreasonable shyness had often annoyed her when she was alive. If their very purpose as flowers was to be seen and admired, why then did they seek invisibility? She would nonetheless spend hours by the pond, waiting for them to appear, as if they were a rarely seen star or planet in the sky, and was thrilled when she finally spotted them emerging into the air. However, nowadays, she empathised with them and understood them better. Some ghosts sought to be seen and acknowledged; others, like her, did not.

She stood still for a moment, simply glad to be here in her favourite place on earth. In the early days of ghosthood, struggling to reconcile with her new avatar, she had been anxious about what would happen to her beloved garden with her passing. The historian had been correct in that regard: she had indeed fled from her homeland, to which she had no hope of returning – and this house and garden would become a recompense for all that she would always miss about her home soil. But with her gone, would they cut down the trees and uproot the flowers from the garden? Would they build ugly structures upon it? She was pleased that the museum authorities had appointed gardeners who had lovingly ensured that her garden remained the paradise she had created and intended it to be. The orange trumpet vine generously smothered the white facade of the house, while a congregation of tropical plants loudly but elegantly registered their presence outside one of the French windows. She had admittedly never cared much for the plants when she was alive, but she now admired their bold patterns and shapes, the way they added to the many stories living inside her garden.

She turned her attention to the trees, many of which she had personally planted; what were once timid saplings now soared high above her, even towering above the house. She made sure to say hello to each of them, wondering: did *they* see her? Did they remember her? It was hard to tell with the trees, though, as they became more and more stoic the older they turned, reluctant to betray emotion. While the majority of them looked to be flourishing, their branches generously embracing the night sky, the poinsettia looked rather forlorn, which made her heart weep. How difficult it had been to grow, how much it had sulked and pouted, she remembered, thinking of all those times when she would steal away to secretly talk to it, persuading it to life, as one would a child refusing to eat. And perhaps her encouraging words had worked, for when it did finally grow, how dramatic had been its transformation, a vivid red cloud in all that green.

She remembered picking up its fallen scarlet feathers of leaves and telling stories about a red-feathered bird who lived in her garden to the children who would visit the house. She could still hear them loudly demanding to see the bird and her telling them that he was very shy and emerged only at night when they were fast asleep. The presence of these little ones in the house and gardens became a great antidote to her loneliness, especially when her husband left her after decades of marriage to start a new life with someone somewhere else. The children's laughter and innocent questions had done much to alleviate her pain and mourning, bringing light to lightless days. She wondered if children ever wandered towards the poinsettia tree anymore; perhaps, the absence of children surrounding it with their curiosity and love was the reason behind the tree's despondency. She wished she had words of encouragement to offer to the tree today, but she did not – and all she could do was to kindly pat its branches before making her way to the rose garden.

Some nights, she avoided going to the rose garden; some nights, she found herself inexorably drawn towards it, like iron filings to a magnet: it had been a twenty-fifth wedding anniversary gift from her husband after they had first moved into the house. 'You are always complaining I don't bring you roses,' he had said, gesturing towards a circle of rumpled earth, 'so I decided to gift you a rose garden instead.'

How much fun and joy she had had in planning the rose garden, what she had once thought of as the most beloved of her husband's gifts. She had secretly chosen the roses for the poetry of their names, rather than their appearance, and yet, when they eventually bloomed, she had loved them all the more for their colours and their fragrances: oh, their magnificent fragrances. She would marvel at how her beloved roses changed colour at dawn and dusk or on full moon nights, as if they were donning different costumes and personalities.

If she could, she would have spent all of her days there, if only she hadn't been worried that the other flowers would feel put out by her playing such obvious favourites with the roses. *I love you all,* she would declare to those flowers, knowing in her heart of hearts that she was uttering a lie.

Love: she thought she had reached that age when she knew all that she had to know of it, only to be proved wrong, so wrong. After her husband left her and their home, without a single backward glance, she had been tempted to uproot the rose garden in her grief and fury. What she had seen as an eternity ring of love had become anything but that; she still recalled with cold shock that terrible morning, seeing his wedding ring on her bedside table, a letter of apology placed beneath it, the objects conveying what he had been unable to do in person. She had torn up the letter, but she had not the heart to dispose of the ring; she eventually kept it inside a cupboard along with all the other things that had once belonged to him and of which she similarly could not rid herself. As for the destruction of the rose garden, the impulse had not stayed for long and she began to see it as a place of memories instead, with extraordinary beauty and decay, soft petals and thorns, and soaring heartbreak and joy nestled within it. And in days to come, it was this rose garden that would become her ultimate refuge and solace, the white space between one chapter and the next.

As she bent to cup a butter-yellow rose in her palm, two white egrets suddenly flew out of the pink trumpet flower tree behind her. They looked like ghosts themselves, phantom paint-strokes upon the blank air. Perhaps they were refugees from the nearby lake who had sought sanctuary here in the garden. She had never seen them before but then she never had been much of a birdwatcher. She watched them settle on the top of the banyan tree, sitting so closely together that they almost became one. She was glad of their presence for they made her feel less alone.

By now, she should have been used to this loneliness, having inhabited that desolate country for so many years both as a ghost and when she was alive. And yet, perhaps, the sad and final truth was that you never did get used to it regardless of how long you had been in that state. After her husband left, she had spent long hours wandering from room to room, wondering why it was that he had decided to share the twilight of his years with someone he had barely known for months. What was it about her that had prompted him to leave her when she needed him the most? There were no answers, there never could be – and yet she kept on asking the plants, the empty chairs, the walls, until their ears became thick from hearing her unanswerable questions. After a while, she simply stopped asking and got on with what remained of her life. She poured more and more of herself into the garden, spending nearly all her waking hours there and returning inside only when the sun bid adieu for the day.

She gazed up at the moon, thinking of those full moon evenings when she had been alive and unable to sleep. She would then go down to the garden, walking around as she was doing now, glimpsing it all drenched in opalescent moonshine and inhaling the fragrance of plants in slumber. *I must do this more often*, she had told herself then, *the garden is as enchanting a place at night as it is during the day*. But even though she tried to prolong staying in the garden as long as she could, sleep would eventually overcome her and she would finally return to her room, slipping back into bed, like a letter into an envelope. But no bed or room beckoned her now: she could stay in the garden all night for she no longer needed to sleep – one of the few recompenses that her ghostly existence afforded her. She saw that the full moon had now occupied its throne in the sky; she turned around and saw the house bathed in the pearly moonlight, looking simultaneously utterly solid and breathtakingly fragile. The sight assuaged the constant homesickness that burned in her heart. *This is the reason why I return again and again*, she whispered, *why I will keep on returning, no matter what.* And she remained rooted there, feeling a surge of such overwhelming, heartbreaking love for her beloved house and garden that she thought that she would be subsumed by it.

For a long while, she had wondered if ghosts too had expiry dates, if ghosts too died, becoming fainter and fainter until one day they simply vanished into the air. She worried less and less about this reality nowadays, just as the idea of not living had ceased to frighten her in the last few years of her life. Her world had whittled down to these two salient truths: inhabiting the air, and regular visits to her house and garden – and truth be told, she honestly did not need anything else. Perhaps, this was what they called contentment: perhaps finding and holding onto these meaningful things was at the heart of what it meant to exist, whether in corporeal or spirit form. She looked at the house for a little longer before switching her gaze to the moon – and this was how she spent the remainder of the night, looping back and forth between the moon and the house until dawn-break.

She customarily waited till the sun rose and the dainty pink hibiscus opened before she said goodbye to the house. When she was alive, she would finish drinking her morning tea and then go down to the garden to pluck the first hibiscus she saw blooming that day. Even though she rarely plucked flowers from the garden, disapproving of those who would succumb to the beauty of a flower and greedily wished to possess it for themselves, she always allowed herself one hibiscus. She would tuck it into her hair, in the mirror of the dressing table, soaking in every moment of its evanescent beauty. And so, after all these years of ghosthood, she continued to pluck the first pink flower she would see emerging from the bush, the sole souvenir she permitted herself to take from her home each time she visited it.

The gardener had already arrived at the house to conduct his work for the day: to coax shy flowers to face the world while gently clipping the wings of those who harboured grandiose ambitions of fleeing the garden. She wondered if he suspected her of being here as had the gardeners before him: sometimes, she had seen him look in her direction, as if he had somehow sensed her presence. But she knew he would never admit or reveal his suspicions to anyone, leaving her free to roam the place.

From the distance, she saw a faint smile cross his face upon encountering the freshly detached hibiscus bud; she fancied him sensing the phantom pink still lingering in the air, knowing that plucked flowers too became ghosts, albeit short-lived ones. He briefly gazed at the bush and then returned to nourishing and caring for the garden, a devotee at his chosen temple of worship. And the ghost princess reluctantly retraced her steps to the air, wondering if tomorrow night would be too soon to visit again.

EMILY – HIDING IN A FLOWER

DIANA POWELL

for Emily Dickinson

– jasmine
   – rose – maple – gentian
     – violets – violet – viola

Jasmine.
She began with jasmine – and stoneroot, a strange coupling … but doesn't remember why. There is so much she can't remember any more. Once upon a time, her mind was as broad as a summer sky. Now, the sky has darkened and shrunk to no more than the square of her bedroom window – still less, when the drapes are drawn, black and fast. And her words – words that would come to her as she … walked through the garden? Tended her plants? As easily as? – as she …? Gone. Gone, with the fug and the pain of the illness, with the tinctures and pills said to remedy it. Gone with …? Gone.

This is all she has left now, of the words – no, there is no book of her words, beyond her feeble hand-stitched caches – of the flowers … yes, something, but not much. This.

A mouldering tome. A precious antique. The meeting of it – yes, she spoke those words once, she thinks – something she loved. To find an old book, coming across it in a library, or lent by a friend. Joy! This one is hers, all hers, Vinnie says. Not just that she owns it, but that she made it. 'Remember'.

'In school. Mount Hoylake. Where we went,' says – Vinnie – as she puts it down on the coverlet – the cover itself a meddling of tiny blooms and leaves – puts her sister's hands to it. Opens to the first clothed page. 'Look!'

'Be careful, though. It's quite delicate. It's old, after all – though not as old as us!'

Yes.

Delicate is how books can be, pages can be, flowers can be – flowers, most of all – the stalk tender, the petals no more than a moth's wing, veined. Velvet … the faltering stamens, a bee's breath of nectar –

These, here, on the pages in front of her … are different. These, as her fingers flit over them – bee, like a bee, golden – like the butterflies, the dragonflies – there is nothing soft. There is – the skin of a dried bulb, wrapped and over-wintered, an autumn leaf sequestered between tree roots on the forest floor. Crisp. Brittle. Crackling and crunching beneath – fingers, as she sets them out to plant, boots, as she walks through them. Careful, yes, she must be. Or, for, if her fingers pressed down, if her fingers followed their outlines, searching in to the sepals, the calyx, the corolla, their heart, they would crumble into dust. To float away into the cloying air of this, her sickroom, joined with the detritus of her body, her flindering skin, her shrivelling hair, her staccato breath. On, into …

Nothingness. Death.

Coming soon. It will be here soon. But no, that's for her. Not for them.

These, these flowers, this, the book, if she is careful as her sister says, will last a while longer. Not forever, but longer than her own fading, failing body. Which is not much, but something.

Jasmine. Would she have recognised it, without its label fixed across it, in her own, neat hand? Latin, but containing the anglicised word within. (Fortunate, that, making sure of it). Or ... without Vinnie's pronouncements. 'Look! See! Jasmine. See, Emily?'

– the life sucked out of it, all of them – no, not sucked, pressed, *she* did it, remembering now, Vinnie reminding now, picking, plucking the flowers, 'Some from the garden, in the old place, the garden we had then; some from our walks about the school grounds; some from ...' – the leaves, pressing them, heavy weights bearing down on them (more heavy tomes, or the school library's book press), no thought that they might be hurt, might scream – for they can scream, can't they? ... plants, for she has heard them – sap squeezed from them, every last drop, until this – brittle (don't touch!) desiccated blooms.

All she has left of her garden, her glasshouse, the woods, even the pots of hyacinth on the window sill are stubborn this year, as if ... they do not want to bear witness.

Sucked jasmine, sipped. Yes, some of her words were of jasmine – sip it, and what?

She raises the book to her lips. No, of course, she mustn't kiss it, taste it, her toxic drool will dissolve it – not even dust will remain, then. But she can smell, can't she? She can do that, for there is this about jasmine, isn't there, its wondrous scent, its headiness, voluptuousness, how it fills your mind, your heart, your soul – and plain, common stoneroot, too – rub its leaves between your fingers, smell its lemon balm – that is surely why she put them together … for their perfume, to send her to … paradise?

And yes, she has done this before, and yes, it comes back to her – clouds clearing, curtains opened, the darkness shifting, light entering her mind (which happens now and then, new pills prescribed, perhaps; rest), how the jasmine, the stoneroot, the exotic plants she nurtured in her glasshouse, that her father made for her – kind father! – would do this. So that she was not where she seemed to be at all … nowhere like it, at all! Far, far, away –

'Today, I have been to the Spice Islands! It is warm on the islands, far warmer than here, in Massachusetts. A wrap-around shawl warmth, and sultry, close to the forest …'

She pulled the collar from her neck, loosened the ties of her dress. Removed her stockings. Her shoes were already gone. She rubbed her feet on the dark, rich earth. The feel of it, her toes digging down deep. It is the same in the garden – how she would push her fingers into the soil, to feel the roots of the plant, to burrow the seed, the bulbs far. Her mother told her to wear gloves, her mother always wore gloves, her mother and Vinnie, both. But she won't. She likes the dirt, she likes the mud and doesn't mind the sink of it, the slurp at the rise of it, up her legs, on her knees, even, if she has knelt, to dig, to weed, to bury deep. She has more of it in the forest – that darker, richer soil, meandering out between the twisted lianas, sucked up from the mirror'd pools. She has more of everything.

The birds … she has been watching the birds. Birds of paradise, they call them. (See! She knew it was paradise she had gone to!) Their colours, matching the colours of the flowers, colours such as she only sees in her glasshouse, too vivid for a northern clime – azure, opal, purple. And their scent – she opened her lungs wide, breathed in the air, swallowed it down, down and there it was …

Here it is …

But. No. There is no smell, here. No matter how close she holds the book to her face – no smell of jasmine or any plant. Perhaps, if she rubs the petals, as she used to do with the stoneroot leaves – but no, she mustn't do that ('careful, Emily, careful!') – Perhaps ... no, the only smell is the smell of the book, an old book, of must and mould from the foxing of the pages, of the mouldering leather, of the horse glue used to bind it, of ... no scent of paradise, at all.

No paradise at all – just this. A book. Her bed. Her bedroom. Her life. Her death.

And yet ... some might say (their neighbours, their friends, their relatives – her family, sometimes, yes, Vinnie has said it, Sue? – no, not beloved Sue) – isn't this the life she has always wanted – the life they all thought she had craved? Meaning that she is a recluse, who hardly leaves her house, let alone Amherst, certainly that she has never left America. (Because of course, they do not know of the Spice Islands. Or the jungles of South America, or the Asian mountains and forest – all the places she has visited, sent there by the scent of her flowers.)

And now, finally, she is hidden completely. No need to hide behind doors, no need to peep behind curtains, no need to send notes, to save conversation, no need for a thick hedge to keep the world out. No need for her to hide among her flowers. Finally, she can go nowhere but here. Nowhere, nothing, nobody – what – not just they, but she – thought she always wanted.

Marigold – iris

– lily. Lily-of-the valley

Crocus, Sweet William

Chrysanthemum

Mayflowers, so small and pink, true to their name.

Orchis

Tulip

They rise and fall past her, with the turning of the pages, the passing of the hours, the days. Vinnie turning them sometimes when she is too frail for even that small task. 'Slowly, carefully, Emily. Let me do it for you.'

They wink at her, wave at her, when she stays her – or Vinnie's – hand. Sometimes they want more, saying 'Hello, it's me! Remember me?' because they meant so much to her. A favourite. She knows there should be no such thing. With family, friends, playing favourites is a dangerous game. She has seen it so many times. Susan ...

But with the plants ... she has had favourites there, though, in truth, they come and go, must, of necessity, change with the season, or else could be lost for months at a time –

Tiger lily, for matching the colour of her hair – iris, because of its rainbow colours, reminding her of rainbows breaking the leaden skies – hyacinths, planted on these windowsills, their beauty sprung from an onion bulb, winter's foil – snow foil, white, a foil, white, like the daisies.

– Daisy. Favourite of all ...?

Here, now, in front of her, fallen to this page – most certainly crying out – Me, me! Emily! – for all their shyness. Such a humble plant, like so many other humble plants, that she has loved as much as the exotics – the exuberant roses and extravagant peonies; the fragile, yet showy poppies. Daisy, moon-faced clover, lying low in the fields, so small, so insignificant – nobodies, like her – so that she would put them into her words, telling how they mattered for the bees, the butterflies, all the insects crowding to them, finding them hidden in the grass, when there is nothing else to be seen. Feeding on them, then being fed on by the birds ... bringing the birds to the garden. Robin. Bobolink. Blackbird. Another joy, another pleasure out of which to make her words. Another part of her garden, along with her flowers – no, not as much as her flowers, in truth, but still ...

Still, daisy, perhaps, yes, best of all. Loved when he called her it – he, her Master – called it by herself in her journal, loving it for its meaning. Innocence. Loyalty, simplicity. Innocent, loyal, simple – Is that how she saw herself? Is that who she is? No? Yes?

There is this, though, for certain – that the daisy wears white, as she does … did. Still does, seeing her nightgown, her bed-jacket, an old woman's clothes, dying woman's clothes … Yes, this is her.

But – her – alive, once, wearing her white dress, white from collar to hem, inside the house, outside the house. Like a nun, they said, she knew they said, heard from the gossip of the maid, or Vinnie, Sue repeating their talk (only the kindest bits from beloved Sue, of course!) or overhearing it herself through the hedge, or across the pulled door. 'We have seen her, working at her gardening, in the middle of the night, dressed in white!' Or, 'See, how she shuts herself away, shuts out the rest of the world. The nun of Amherst!'

Virgin? Did they ask that, too? Their prying, their gossiping not reaching that far. They do not know of … what? Who?

'Why?' they wonder. 'Why does she do this? Why does she wear white? How does someone who wears white work in the mud and the soil?' Her long skirts dragging in the grime, picking up the dirt, frilled in grey at the bottom, then – *she* has wondered that, too! Why everything?

And yes, she does – did – that, tend her flower beds by moonlight, loving the quiet of it, the light that bathed her and the soil and the plants, her, in her white, shining the moon's light back in return. The peace of it (not knowing of the neighbours' prying eyes, then). And … something she was sure of, though science did not say it, science not having the proof it always demanded … how the flowers planted under the eye of the moon flourished best of all. Perhaps …

Something else she liked, to go out in the snow once it had settled on the ground. For white against white, she is unseen.

One of winter's few pleasures, for, otherwise, she hated the season, for taking her flowers away.

True, she found beauty in a frosted garden – the way the ice, the frost, a gentle dusting of snow, made patterns on all they kissed. The ferns, the leaves – looked at closely – their fronds, their veins – a coating of sugar. But too much, and it kills – could kill her lungs, too, Father said. Said she must stop this, her gardening in winter, reminding her of all who had died of the disease, their breathing stopped, like her breathing stopped. Growing heavy, first, coming in gasps, the cold swallowed down. She tried to hide it, but couldn't in the end … no wonder she must stay in, more and more.

Until …

'Look!'

Daisy –

white, like her. A white flower. Those who do not garden do not understand the uses of white flowers – how they act as a foil against the other colours, to make them stand out more. White as the moon, white as the snow, that frost, summer clouds, white as her dress, newly pulled from the lye, white …

Turned to yellow-grey, on a page of yellow-grey. No longer white, at all.

Colour drained, strength sapped, shape lost, flesh wasted – daisy, jasmine, lilac, zinnia, nasturtium … her. HER! What kind of life is this? Not what she wanted, wants, after all – not without the flowers – not without the words. No life, at all.

Death would be better. She must be glad that it won't be long. She is no stranger to death. All those who have gone there before her, so many that she has loved. (Flowers, again! She sent the bereaved posies, along with her sympathy. They would know the meaning of the flowers, if not the essence of her words.)

All those unknown, killed in the war … dying the worst of deaths, she had heard, so that she should be grateful for *this* – to die in her bed, in her home. Her loved ones around. So much better than a battlefield's killing, flesh torn apart, swimming in blood … alone. Such a dark time – strange, then, that she had put together so many of her best words through those cruel years, as if the nightmare fuelled her. No, not that, no. She will not let it be so.

Let it be, rather, that her plants had taught her. Making her accustomed to the darkness. For she had faced, endured it so many times. For all her care, her love, the moon's blessing – there were those that did not survive. 'Nature,' her mother would say – that there are not only kind bees, kissing butterflies, gentle birds – but enemies, too. Slugs, snails, no matter how she would try to protect from them, with scattered egg shells or raised beds. Caterpillars, of those same glorious butterflies, their jaws munching their way through the petals, the stalks. Gone. Planted one day, next day … gone. That beautiful frost, lasting too long, delving too deep. A precious plant no more. Annuals – nature in them, then, the seed they cast to bring themselves back, eaten, or blown away.

And yet … and yet … they come again. As many of them. Did she not write once that to love flowers meant rebirth each day?! Did she not write that, each morn, they peep out again, prancing? Did she? Please! Or – each year – the hidden bulbs, lost till the spring. The perennials, the earth bare around them. The seed that survives or is gathered to plant again. The rose, the shrubs, the trees – seemingly no more than a dead twig, until the buds sprout again. The violets – her precious, cherished violets, her favourite of favourites, maybe, appearing so early, so low in the fields, unsuspecting, the first sign of the coming spring. Brave little things! The joy that gives. The hope it gives – not just a feathered thing. A coloured thing. Fixed, but floating in the breeze. Growing. A paradise held in a hand. A flower.

Death, overcome.

And here they still are – changed, beyond knowing, reduced to this, but still here. Wasn't that why she had done this – to make them immortal? Telling her friends to do the same? To dry them, press them, fasten them in a book, 'and they will live again!'

– not much – perhaps not forever – but something.

Better, more, than her …

Yes, she will certainly be nobody, soon. No body – so, nobody. No body, no soul, for she does not believe in resurrection. Others, most, here, do. Vinnie, of course, believing in the faith since they were children, but not her. All that will happen is that she will go into the ground, to make food for the flowers … No paradise at all.

Roses – sweet peas – pinks.

Lilies.

Which shall it be – for her funeral?

Should she choose now, and tell Vinnie? Or leave it to her, to them? To her sister, her brother, Mabel, upstart Mabel, Susan – if anyone should choose, she would like it to be Susan, just as she wants Susan to have her words. But no, she wants it to be her own decision. So she will tell Susan, tell her how she wants it to be. 'Dress me in white like my daisies. Put me in a coffin of white, as if I am lost in the snow! Put violets around my bier!' Yes, violets she claims for her own, for her death.

And yes, here it is – here they are, on the page in front of her, now. An array of them, some holding their yellow, three colours dimmed to two, leaves ovate, leaves lobed, lance-shaped, pinnate. Her violas.

She touches them. She cannot help it. Vinnie is not here to stop her. She mimics the picking of each, as she would do to make a posy – remembers that daguerreotype of herself, holding them.

She raises the book to her lips, and kisses them. As she used to do, lying down in the grass in the field, spying them there. And for this moment, it does not matter that they do not feel the same, look the same, smell the same. What matters is that she has not forgotten. They have done what they have always done – brought *her* back to life. And, perhaps, one day, her words that speak of them, telling nature's news, will find some pages of their own, and do the same.

Perhaps ...

– rhododendron – alyssum
  Privet
  Crocus
  gilly flowers
    Hemlock foxglove
  Marigolds
  daffodil, hiding beneath its yellow bonnet.

– jasmine

So many flowers, so many plants. Year after year, life after life. Page after page, on and on. She counts them, as others count sheep. Until she sleeps.

CLEMATIS 'LASURSTERN', *Clematis*

STITCHING FOR CLEM

ELIZABETH GIBSON

1: Foxglove

The first time I saw you, I had been hiking, and everything was pink with foxgloves. The fells were like quartz, and it felt magical, like if I looked too hard or breathed too loudly, it would all vanish and leave just green hills again. So, I kept believing, and believing … and stumbled on a root. I cried out, then tried to rein it in – drawing attention to myself terrified me back then. But the line of queer women hikers all stopped and looked back. 'All right?'

I nodded, walked determinedly forward, my ankle throbbing. The group turned back to face the front but, as we went, I got a few quick side-glances, half-smiles, checking I was really okay. A kindness, that I tried to let soak into me. I was still getting my head around there being so many people who were like me, and yet all so different. And that I was welcome to walk with them.

It didn't come easy to me. I could sit in my room all day, and do art, and feel things very deeply, and sometimes I did just need to do that, to reconnect with something inside me. But then, I could also choose to go out hiking, and know that we all had this one, intimate, core thing in common. It shone between us, across ages and jobs, or whether we were confident, or shy like me. It was this otherworldly glow, like the foxgloves.

Back at the youth hostel, some of us sat and watched the lake, the sky, and the resting boats shift from blue to silver to dark. I gently massaged my foot. Someone from another group had found a guitar, and it was being passed around, mainly between guys, who gave loud renditions of Oasis. Then, someone stepped out of nowhere, all broad frame, patchwork jacket, windswept honey-coloured hair. She started to play. You started to play, Clem.

I closed my eyes and *felt* your voice, deep and full, like cream, but with an edge. A challenge. Opening my eyes, I watched your deft fingers, and remembered – from my keen gardener Mam – that the foxglove's Latin name, *Digitalis*, means fingers. Your fingers were strong and tanned, not pink or dainty at all, but still, there was something of the foxglove there. The myth of it, maybe. The brightness in the dark.

I remembered also that foxgloves are used in drugs that treat heart conditions. And then, you sang, '... *my heart*'. The final words of the song, drawn out, low and long. We were both living within the word 'heart' at that moment when you looked right across and saw me. It all felt meant to be.

Now, I stitch quickly. This is what *my* fingers are good at. Sketching, painting, stitching. I can't play an instrument. I've tried, and it sounds terrible, and you laugh at me as kindly as you can, and tell me – with that foxglove glow in your eye – to put my fingers to better use. When you are here, it is easy. When you are out, as you are now, I stitch flowers.

Each foxglove is a joy: rich, mauve-coloured thread for the bells, with tiny flecks of darker red for the pollen. As I stitch, I smell hills, recent rain, damp clothes. I can hear every woman in the group: her story, and life advice, and laughter. I can see the old guitar, the pale wood, your honey hair, the taut strings. The way you were so solid, and in your arms, the music was safe, and so could I be.

I can still smell and see and taste the rest of that night, as we talked and talked, by the lake and then on a wooden bunk in my blessedly single room. The guitar had returned to its owner, but you showed me how to make music.

You had asked me my name, out on the deck.

'It's … Grace.'

Your beam, never away for long, peeled across your face. 'That fits you just right.'

And in that moment, I knew someone out there was gracing me with something. That was the beginning.

2: Honeysuckle

My great aunt made me one of these samplers, for my baptism day. Stitched ducklings and daffodils and bluebells, with my being born in March (I'm a classic Pisces, you say. You are, of course, a fiery Sagittarius). From when I was just 5 or 6, admiring the sampler in Mam's bedroom, I resolved, *I will make one of these for someone's baby, someday.*

Things were quiet at home. We lived in a largish town, but I was seen as a loner and a nerd, and no one at school wanted to hang out with me at the weekends. I just snuggled in at home and did arts and crafts. Sometimes, Mam and I would meander out to the market and chat with the lady on the craft stall, to get me bits and pieces to make my next creations. One time, we found some shimmery pink-gold fabric like a sunset, and I was incredibly happy.

Fast-forward twenty years, and I was venturing out, meeting with my social groups, catching the train around the North to hike, staying in hostels, though never sharing with anyone. I was still very self-contained. I worked in computer programming, as my mind liked the patterns and logic and, as I did it all remotely, I barely needed to leave the house.

Then came the foxglove night, and you hurtled into my neatly crafted life. Suddenly, all my threads were unpicked, my drawings soaked, becoming abstract and gorgeous.

You lived in Manchester, the bee city. You would come and visit me, my weekends now full to bursting with our adventures, my weeknights so lonely. We talked and talked on the phone.

Mam said, 'Go on, go and be with her. I'll survive on my own.'

I was surprised we had been so obvious to her. I hadn't even really come out to her – she just knew I was hiking with groups of women, not the queer part.

She rolled her eyes when I said so. 'Look at your hair.'

I had chopped it all off, after wanting to for years. 'That doesn't mean I fancy Clem ...'

She snorted, then her eyes crinkled in a rare moment of simple, pure warmth. 'It means you seem like you are finally the person you were always meant to be. Go. Spread your wings ... You're nearly thirty, for Pete's sake.' The moment was gone, her eyes back to their usual affectionate exasperation.

The big city scared me. I liked being *here*, with my cosy bed and chair, all my art supplies, and Mam and her prized roses and jasmine.

But you told me about your garden; well, the garden of the house you shared with two other postgrad students in the suburbs. You said it was full of honeysuckle, and the evenings smelt so sweet. You said in Manchester, we could walk the canals and parks, we could eat food from anywhere in the world, we could go to libraries and museums and craft fairs.

'There are so many art shops in the Northern Quarter,' you said. 'You can buy absolute rainbows of threads and yarns, and sequins and beads, and tiny jingle bells ...' Of course, with you, it always came back to music.

I found a little place near you. I could afford to live alone, but I never had done, and the worry gnawed at me that first day as you helped me to carry my things from the bus (neither of us drove). After dumping everything in my fairly ordinary first-floor flat, we headed to your house, where the others had (very considerately) gone out. You showed me your room up in the attic, and all your instruments: guitar, mandolin, ukelele, tin whistle. I held each like a sacred artefact, and they glowed in the late golden light.

We sat out in the garden, under the honeysuckle, and the scent was glorious. At one point, a quick breeze came and knocked a pink-gold wheel of flower right against my lips. 'It's kissing you,' you said. 'It's welcoming you to the honey city, the land of bees. On my bee-half.' You smirked at your wit.

I wiped happy tears from my eyes as you blew on your tin whistle, picked out the Irish folk songs you had learnt secretly for tonight. My Mam's family came from Ireland. I often felt very detached from it all, like something had been lost. Now, you brought it back to me.

I stitch every colour of honeysuckle: golden, cream, white, that hint of pink. The colour of a sunset in the Manchester suburbs, the colour of your playing my past and future on a golden whistle, every note perfect.

When the garden was dark blue and full of midges, you led me back inside. You took over from the honeysuckle at my mouth, and I took over from the whistle at yours.

3: Violets

I learnt so much about you, dear Clem. That you loved violet creams, and strawberry creams, and anything that is just sugar inside dark chocolate. I would slip them into your bag or under your pillow. Your rugged outer layer was so reddish and earthy, that this inner part of you that loved granny chocolates – the sweet tooth, the purple-pink spark – was precious, like the inside of a geode. I tried my best to keep it safe and unchanged.

And yet, things had to change. You had laughingly called yourself an eternal student, but you finally had to graduate with your second degree, in music, and look for work. You found it so hard. You envied me having a solid skill – programming – as I could take it with me anywhere and no one would dispute my ability at it. I thought, *it isn't that simple to be me, Clem.* But I didn't say it. I could see the ache in you.

You got an entry-level office job, admin and marketing stuff. You were older than everyone else on your team, and while the women were always impeccably manicured, hair blow-dried, you were as rough-and-ready as ever. You were always big: tall, broad, your middle soft. Your hair was weathered from your travels, and bleached from the sun. You told me you felt like an ugly rough rock among gems. You started trying to diet, which made you teary and slow. I missed you bounding about the place.

One day, I took you for a mystery walk. We took the bus to north Manchester, to a land of old factories and warehouses and railway bridges. I used to go to the retail park there to get some of my tech stuff and, one day, I saw a cat wandering about and decided to follow it. It led me down a road draped with whispering trees, past the River Irk and its wild green valley, to this big mound of earth. The cat slipped away, and I stood, amazed at this place that was here all along.

Now I moved my sweaty palm from your eyes and you looked around. All was soft and curved – I suspected we were standing among artificial hills from the filling in of a mine or quarry. You took it all in: the Manchester skyline in the distance. A blue balloon of sky. Golden stalks of grass, like corn. Dog roses, and hawthorn blossom and – yes, violets. The ground seemed to hum under our feet. A sacred space. A fairyland.

I led you to a collection of squarish stones at the top, and we sat – well, you quickly eased yourself to sprawling on the warm, pulsing earth. You looked so peaceful, finally. I pulled off your shoes, and you smiled ruefully up at me. 'Sorry for being a sad thing,' you said.

I touched your hair. 'You are the most ancient and magical thing here,' I murmured, hoping you would believe it. Hoping you would feel my heartbeat, like your hand on the guitar strings that you hadn't touched in months.

You slid me down next to you, and we arched into each other's warmth, looking up at the swollen silver moon that had appeared in the sky. Night fell, and moths whirred. Bats fluttered. You sighed in utter contentment as the constellations began to emerge in the exposed circle of sky.

In the dark, my hand stole to your tight workpants, undid the buttons, eased them open, then smoothed your shirt out over your perfect planet of belly. I felt the deep, sore grooves from the waistband and buttons. You'd thought wearing a size too small would help you to eat less. My heart squeezed for you, and I kissed your cheek.

We lay for what felt like hours, my palm orbiting your navel, you snuggling your nose into my neck. 'I need to get some bottoms that fit,' you announced at last, and I knew you were blushing purple. We dragged ourselves to our feet and took the bus home. You led me to your room and picked up your guitar.

4: Poppies

From the cool purply-blue threads of the violets, I move towards the reds and oranges and yellows I have laid out for my poppy collection. The colour of flowers, and also of blood, in its varying phases of drying out.

Blood is no longer my nemesis.

There was a time when I was a teenager that I kept feeling faint and dizzy, and they sent me to have blood taken. I made the mistake of looking, and ... I didn't like it. I honestly thought well into my thirties that I would never be able to have blood drawn again, and I had no idea what I would do if I got ill and needed it.

What was wrong with you in the end? With the faintness? I hear your voice in my head.

Just low in iron, I reply.

That's easy to fix, you tease, *now that you have conquered your blood phobia.*

I laugh, as I dance the needle around my fingers.

How could you have had issues with blood, and had embroidery as your chief hobby? You ponder.

I shrug. *I just never stabbed myself. I was too good at it, from a young age.*

Show off. Your radiant ghost-self strides out, chuckling.

You had always had your GP in the city centre, near your university, and then near your work. When you started having pins and needles in your hand and fingers, especially after tearing up a storm on one of your many stringed instruments (you had now added a banjo and a twelve-string guitar to your collection), you trundled into town to the doctor and described your problem, thinking they would set you some physio exercises.

Instead, you were told that you almost definitely had a wonky nerve in your elbow, and would need surgery on it. You were told you could be treated for free at a private hospital, because they had a bed (a whole individual room in fact!), and you could have it all over within a few months.

You called me to come to you. I made my quick way to Manchester, then we walked all the way back, south, from loud to quiet, towers to houses. You told me *you* had a mystery place to show *me* this time, but to not cover my eyes because there was a lot of traffic. Curious, I followed you to an island in the middle of big grey roads.

It was like we were in a portal to another, softer version of the world. There were wildflowers up to our waists: white and yellow daisies, blue cornflowers, red poppies. You sat me down, and I imagined that to the people driving past, we were invisible. I hoped we were.

We were at the age where most of the people we had known at school had already had their kids. I kind of thought, because we weren't interested in that, we could have a peaceful life, reasonably free of hospital gowns, and hospital food, and blood.

We could sit forever in your white-and-blue garden – your housemates had moved on now; it really was all yours – and talk, and eat the pasta we had cooked, and you could make music, and I could make art, and it would all be calm.

But here we were, with all these red poppies. And they seemed like they were meant to be here, were part of the bigger picture. 'Do you have to have it done?' I asked.

'I could wait and see if it gets worse, which it probably will. I don't want to risk it. I couldn't bear never being able to play an instrument again.'

I nodded. I couldn't bear it either if you had to suffer such a loss.

We got up and backed out of the wildflowers, carefully righting the stalks we had squashed on the way in. On the edge of the road, we looked back. We might never have been there at all. I wondered how many others had done the same as us.

You had the surgery.

I wasn't allowed to be in your room with you, but I waited downstairs in the hospital foyer. You kept me up to date by text. When you said, *I'm going in now*, I think my heart stopped. I curled in a ball for the next twenty minutes. A few staff walking past asked if I was okay. I made a grunting kind of yes.

You texted me to say you were awake, and I sat and cried. I felt like I'd been through something huge, when it wasn't major surgery, and wasn't even me it was happening to. You said they were feeding you well, and I was glad. *Eat, eat*, I told you.

Oh, I'm eating, you replied. I wiped my eyes, laughing in relief.

I never got to see you in your hospital gown or slippers. You reappeared with a nurse an hour or so later, dressed back in your own clothes and coat. It was like the thing you just went through may never have happened, and I would never really understand it. I wondered if this was what it was like for people to watch their partner have a baby.

I came and took your arm from the nurse, led you out towards the bus stop. You were walking normally, were totally lucid. 'I'm not even tired,' you said. 'I feel like I've had a really good night's sleep.'

On the bus, I finally asked to look at your bandage. I felt so shy, like I was peeling off your clothes for the first time. You slid off your coat, and we looked at it together: white, neat, not a hint of blood or of what had just happened to your body underneath it.

That night, you had a shower – you couldn't bear not to, though you were meant to be keeping the bandage dry. A stain the colour of tea rippled over the cloth. I felt faint, but I knew fainting was out of the question. My role here tonight was to stay and watch over you.

But you were fine. Life was surprisingly normal. Your bandage accumulated stains in every shade of poppy, but when we went back to show the nurse, she said it was okay. The blood sometimes had to come out, or it would be all swollen inside.

She snipped off the dressing with scissors and cleaned your scar. Again, I felt like a voyeur, looking at this new part of your body. The stitches were heavy and black, like a zip holding you together (I probably could have done a neater job). But the scar looked like it would be small.

'Touch it,' you said one day, when it was healing. You guided my hand, and I rested it on your fleshy golden upper arm, then eased it downwards. 'Here,' you said, handing me the oil you had been using to massage it.

I plopped some onto my palm – again, this all felt so weirdly intimate – and rubbed it in. You didn't flinch.

'What do you feel?' I asked.

'Physically? Nothing,' you said. 'But I have you here, so inside, I feel … red. Good red.'

I tie off the thread on my final poppy. Of course. You have always been red to me, warm and fiery and vital. Why should your blood scare me? Why should mine? What a gift you are to me, Clem.

5: Wild Clematis

I always used to worry that I was missing out on some life I could and should have had. I expected to have got out of the city long ago, moved to a town like Mam, bought a house. I kept thinking there was some happy ending to work towards, though I wasn't sure what. Not having kids. Not being super-rich. But surely *something.*

And yet … our life was so sweet. Working, renting – in the same house now, at last – and spending our time together in this brilliant, quick, buzzing city. Going on hiking trips, with a group, or just us. You playing at open mic nights in bars, or sessions at Irish pubs. Me entering my paintings and samplers into community art shows. We never hit the big time, but that was never really the plan.

I always vowed I would make an embroidered sampler for someone's baby, and you are my baby, Clem. Your name is Clementine, tough on the outside, sweet and nourishing within, a whole golden world to cup in my hands. You once poked at the fancy clematis variants in my Mam's garden – blue dancer, pink flamingo, purple haze – and said a part of you still wished you could be like that, that Clem could be short for Clematis without it being laughable.

I said, 'How many years do I have to keep loving you, and feeding you, and grinning like a Cheshire cat whenever you enter a room, for you to accept that you are my everything? That if you didn't exist, and some other person did who looked like a flamingo – well, I would be nice to them, of course, but oh, Clem, how I would wish they were citrussy and round.'

Then, I reminded you of that day, when you were working, and I was walking back from Salford, where I had been part of an exhibition in an old shopping unit. It was spring, and the walk would be an hour at least, but I wanted to feast on everything I love: the temperate air, the yellow goslings in the canals, the blossoms falling like confetti.

I felt buoyant. I was getting to the point in life where I was called an *older woman* by some of the twenty-somethings at your gigs or in hiking groups. I never let my hair grow out, which I had once seen as some kind of queer woman's rite of passage. I just liked it short. I still wore T-shirts and men's jeans, nothing fancy at all. I almost felt like I had stepped outside of time.

I remembered long ago, the hills covered in shining pink foxgloves. I think that was my first look into this other timeline, this other way to live, where there were so many possibilities.

On a warm street in Salford, I stopped to drag my water bottle from my backpack – another thing I couldn't quite grow out of – and leant against a red-brick wall covered in white flowers. They were strangely familiar, like something I knew when I was very young, but couldn't name. I sent Mam a photo. She was past her gardening years now, but she was still completely on-it when it came to identifying flowers and berries and fungi.

She came back with, *Surely YOU know?* And even managed a winking face.

No, I said. *Is it Grace-flower? Is that a thing?*

She sent some rolling-around-laughing faces. When I gave her that phone, I created a monster.

It's a wild clematis, she said. *The only one that is native to here, that isn't cultivated like mine.*

I blinked. I reached out to touch its soft flowers. It was like a cloud. I rested my cheek on it.

Now, I stitch each fluffy white flower, a glut of stars, pouring out light into the cosmos. This is the clematis that I can see you in, and that I can see in you.

I stand back from my handiwork. There are music notes and clementines, bees and bats, the curves of hills in the background. There are no dates or birth weights, no numbers at all. Just flowers and flowers. I can almost smell them, waves of perfume lifting from the threads.

The door creaks open, and there you are, and how has it been twenty years? Your hair is silver and gold now, your hands more calloused than ever from those strings. Your face is creased with rivers and roads and straggly stems. I hold up my creation. For once, neither of us has any words.

Then you say, 'Where will we put it?'

And I say, 'We'll bring it wherever we go,' because I know we can. Whatever comes next. However many more hospitals may be involved, whatever the loss or grief – and with Mam getting older, and many of our friends getting ill as happens at our age, those things are inevitable. However much we change. We will have ourselves and our wildflowers.

The first time I saw you, I had been hiking, and everything was pink with foxgloves. The last time I see you, I want to be aware of every colour and scent and every piece of music and magic around us.

Now, I step up to you, drinking in that old swagger, that bashful smile, your stocky form, every inch for me to tend to, to help grow. Right until the very end. We will never stop growing.

NOTES

'Breathing Becoming Midori'. Poem and translation by Aulic Anamika.

'Dog Roses' was first published online in Fictive Dream.

'Flowers' was first published in the Bristol Short Story Prize Anthology, 2015.

ACKNOWLEDGEMENTS

I would like to thank Nicola Guy and her colleagues at The History Press for their help and expertise. To the many writers who submitted their work to this anthology, it was a pleasure reading your words. Special thanks to Barbara Clark, the contributors for sharing their wonderful stories and to Sarah Jane Humphrey for designing the exquisite artwork for this book. My love and thanks to Adam, Iris, and Lauren Drouet for their unfailing love, encouragement, and support of my writing.

THE CONTRIBUTORS

Aulic Anamika

Aulic Anamika (she/they) is a post-migrant writer of colour with South Asian heritage. Apart from science fiction she writes poetry, literary fiction, creative nonfiction, and stand-up tragedies. In 2022 she founded the Queer*ing Creative Writing Group (QCWG) in Berlin.

Aulic writes, 'I had never been a plant person. Then the Covid-19 pandemic happened. It was hard not to notice the subtle movements of my houseplant. This story embodies the speculative imagination of post-migrant human-plant relations.'

Mark Bowers

Mark could be described as a smudge you can't get rid of. Raised in England and preoccupied with Italy and Shakespeare, he is currently wrestling an obsession with the Botanical Gardens of Padua. Mark's botanical stories are the product of grasping the nettle.

'A Clear View' illustrates how his interests in phytosociology, seventeenth-century herbals and random synchronicities are compromised by a fluttery butterfly mind.

Maria Donovan

Award-winning writer Maria Donovan lives in Dorset. Her debut novel, *The Chicken Soup Murder*, was a finalist for the Dundee International Book Prize and her flash fiction story, 'Aftermath', won the Bridport Prize. Read more about Maria on www.mariadonovan.com

The story 'Narcissus' was inspired by her experiences as an immigrant to the Netherlands. It seeks to share some of that inside knowledge with the reader, while maintaining a tight story about a person whose main focus is on her own reflection.

Hildegard Dumper

Hildegard was born and lived in Malaysia and Singapore till she was 16. Currently living in the UK, Hildegard continues to visit the region regularly. Now retired, she is concentrating on her writing while also creating a wildlife-friendly garden.

Hildegard writes, 'Family holidays were spent walking in the jungle. Discovering monkey cups was always a delight. In this short story I wanted to describe the jungle I had known and pay tribute to the people living there who I met.'

Rebecca Ferrier

Rebecca Ferrier is an award-winning writer based in Edinburgh and author of *The Salt Bind* (due for publication in 2025 by Renegade). Her recent prose has been published by *Extra Teeth* and *New Gothic Review*, while her poetry can be found in *Poetry Ireland Review* (139) and *The Friday Poem*. She is represented by Alex Cochran at C&W.

Rebecca writes, "Mulch' was inspired by the invisibility of a woman's needs in our contemporary society. Often, our use is placed in youth and beauty, with our wisdom and desires rarely considered once we reach a certain age.'

Elizabeth Gibson

Elizabeth writes stories, poems, and theatre. She has worked with Manchester Literature Festival, Manchester Poetry Library, Manchester Pride, the Portico Library, Oldham Coliseum, and Yorkshire Dance, and has been published in *Confingo*, *Lighthouse, Magma, Popshot, Spelt, Strix*, and *Under the Radar*. elizabeth-gibson.com

Elizabeth writes, 'I wanted to write a queer Manchester love story full of hope and happiness, including some of my favourite places where the city and nature come together, as well as my passions for hiking, music and art.'

Thalia Henry

Thalia Henry lives in Auckland, in Aotearoa, New Zealand, but she grew up on the South Island Otago coast. She is the author of the novel *Beneath Pale Water*.

Thalia was inspired to write *Nigella* after looking at *Nigella sativa* on the window sill of her mother's home in the coastal town of Karitane. The seedpods reminded her of little hearts. www.thaliahenry.com

Tamar Hodes

Tamar Hodes is a retired teacher for whom fiction writing is a passion. Her novels are *Raffy's Shapes*, *The Water and the Wine* and *Mixed*, while some of her short stories are collected in *The Watercress Wife and Other Stories*.

Dog roses are dear to Tamar. They even featured on her wedding cake forty years ago! Her story explores the struggles between conformity and rebellion, the tame and the wild, and obedience and resistance. Tamar has questions but no answers.

Sarah Jane Humphrey

Sarah's talent and distinctive style has made her a coveted illustrator within her field. She is an award-winning artist with four RHS medals from one of the most prestigious botanical art exhibitions in the world. In 2023 she accepted the gold medal awarded for her collection of seaweed paintings at the Saatchi Gallery in London. Much of her work is published in books and editorials. Sarah's portfolio includes commissions for an array of clients including the Royal College of Physicians, BrewDog, The Eden Project, the Duchy of Cornwall, and Jo Malone.

Diana Powell

Diana Powell is the winner of several short story prizes. Her novella, *The Sisters of Cynvael*, won the Cinnamon Press Literature Award and will be published next year.

Her novel, *things found on the mountain* (Seren Books) is out now.

Diana writes, 'Hope is the thing with feathers' ... or the violet, the daisy, the rose – things found in Emily Dickinson's garden that taught her resilience and inspired her work. And those poems, echoing my own love of nature, inspired me, too.'

Clare Reddaway

Clare writes short stories and plays. Recent highlights include being longlisted for the BBC National Short Story Awards and shortlisted for the Bridport Prize. Her novella *Dancing in the Shallows* will be published by Fairlight Books in 2024.

Clare writes, 'My sister gave me an acorn vase one Christmas. I found the perfect specimen while tramping the lanes of Wales. Watching that acorn sprout and grow roots in front of my eyes was an engrossing, contemplative, and, it turns out, inspiring experience.'

Priyanka Sacheti

Priyanka Sacheti is a writer from Bangalore, India. Her writing has appeared in many literary journals such as *Barren, Dust Mag Poetry, Common, Popshot, Lunchticket* and various anthologies. She is working on a poetry collection and can be found on Twitter @priyankasacheti.

Priyanka writes, 'The inspiration for this story is a beautiful colonial building in Bangalore, where I live. The structure's interesting history, distinctive architecture and verdant garden made me imagine one of its former inhabitants as a ghost revisiting her beloved former home.'

Angela Sherlock

Stories from Angela's collection about the Irish diaspora have been published in literary journals and anthologies, and other work has appeared in online magazines. *The Garden of the Non-Completer Finisher* comes from a collection upon which she is currently working, which takes its themes from the elements of the periodic table.

Angela writes, 'My own garden was the inspiration for this story. The high walls send plants tumbling drunkenly out of the borders, chasing the sunlight. And I never quite finish tidying up.' www.angelasherlock.com

Kate Swindlehurst

A graduate of the creative writing MA at Anglia Ruskin University, Kate Swindlehurst lives in Cambridge. She has written novels and short fiction. *The Tango Effect*, her memoir exploring the impact of Argentine tango on Parkinson's disease, was published by Unbound in 2020.

Kate writes, 'Whilst writer-in-residence at Cambridge University Botanic Garden, I learnt about the hidden properties of plants. This inspired the creation of Mercy, a nineteenth-century herbalist who relies on her expertise for survival.'

Emma Timpany

Emma is a writer from the far south of Aotearoa, New Zealand, who loves flowers, plants, and short stories. Her books include *Three Roads* (Red Squirrel Press), *Travelling in the Dark* (Fairlight Books) and *Cornish Short Stories* (co-editor, The History Press).

Her story grew from a love of flowers, botany, and gardening, and her years as a florist and flower grower in New Zealand and England. The wild beauty of the Otago Peninsula and south-east Cornwall inspired the story's setting.

Find out more about our contributors, news, and events at www.botanicalshortstories.uk
Twitter @BotanicalShorts
Instagram @botanicalshortstories